FRANKÉTIENNE

Ready to Burst

Translated from the French by Kaiama L. Glover

archipelago books

First Archipelago Books Edition, 2014

First published as *Mûr à crever* by Ana Editions, 2004.

Library of Congress Cataloging-in-Publication Data
Frankétienne.
[Mûr à crever. English]
Ready to Burst / Frankétienne ; translated from the French by Kaiama L. Glover. –
First Archipelago Books edition.
pages cm
ISBN 978-1-935744-78-8 (paperback) – ISBN 978-1-935744-79-5 (e-book)
I. Glover, Kaiama L., 1972- translator. II. Title.
PQ3949.2.F7M87 2014
843'.914–dc23   2014025484

Archipelago Books
232 Third Street, #A111
Brooklyn, NY 11215
www.archipelagobooks.org

Distributed by Random House
www.randomhouse.com

Cover art: Frankétienne
Book design by David Bullen

Archipelago Books is grateful for the generous support of Lannan Foundation,
the National Endowment for the Arts, and the New York State Council on the Arts,
a state agency. Cet ouvrage publié dans le cadre du programme d'aide à la publication
bénéficie du soutien du Ministère des Affaires Etrangères et du Service de l' Ambassade
de France représenté aux Etats-Unis. This work received support from the French
Ministry of Foreign Affairs and the Cultural Services of the French Embassy in the
United States through their publishing program.

Printed in the United States of America

Ready to Burst

M ORE EFFECTIVE at setting each twig aquiver in the passing of waves than a pebble dropped into a pool of water, Spiralism defines life at the level of relations (colors, odors, sounds, signs, words) and historical connections (positionings in space and time). Not in a closed circuit, but tracing the path of a spiral. So rich that each new curve, wider and higher than the one before, expands the arc of one's vision.

In perfect harmony with the whirlwind of the cosmos, the world of speed in which we evolve, from the greatest of human adventures to struggles for liberation, Spiralism aligns perfectly – in breadth and depth – with an atmosphere of explosive vertigo; it follows the movement that is at the very heart of all living things. It is a shattering of space. An exploding of time.

Re-creating wholes from mere details and secondary materials, the practice of Spiralism reconciles Art and Life through literature, and necessarily breaks with the hypocrisy of the Word. Re-cognition. Totality.

In this sense, as a means of expression – efficient, *par excellence* – Spiralism uses the Complete Genre, in which novelistic description, poetic breath, theatrical effect, narratives, stories, autobiographical sketches, and fiction all coexist harmoniously . . .

■ ■ ■

Every day, I employ the dialect of untamed hurricanes. I speak the madness of opposing winds.

Every evening, I use the patois of furious rains. I speak the rage of overflowing waters.

Every night, I speak to the islands of the Caribbean in the language of hysterical storms. I speak the madness of the sea in heat.

Dialect of hurricanes. Patois of rains. Language of storms. Unfolding of life in a spiral.

In its essence, life is tension. Toward something. Toward someone. Toward oneself. Toward the point of maturation where the ancient and the new unravel. Death and birth. And every being finds itself – in part – in pursuit of its double. A pursuit that might even seem to bear the intensity of need, of desire, of infinite quest.

Dogs pass by (I've always been obsessed with stray dogs). They yap at the silhouette of the woman I've been chasing. At the image of the man I've been seeking out. At my double. At the murmurings of fleeting voices. For so many years now. It feels like thirty centuries.

The woman has left. Without fanfare. Left my heart out of tune. The man never held out his hand to me. My double is always just a step ahead of me. And the unhinged throats of nocturnal dogs let loose terrifying howls, making the sound of a broken accordion.

It is then that I become a tempest of words, bursting open the hypocrisy of clouds and the deceitfulness of silence. Rivers. Storms. Flashes of lightning. Mountains. Trees. Lights. Rains. Untamed oceans. Take me away in the frenzied marrow of your joints. Take me away! It would take just a hint of clarity for me to be born with nine lives. For me to accept life. Tension. The inexorable law of maturation. Osmosis and symbiosis. Take me away! It would take just the sound of a footstep, a glance, a tender voice, for me to live happily in the hope that Man is capable of awakening. Take me away! For it would take so little for me to speak of the sap that circulates in the marrow of cosmic joints.

Dialect of hurricanes. Patois of rains. Language of storms. I speak the unfolding of life in a spiral.

■　■　■

In wanting so desperately to speak, I've become no more than a screaming mouth. I no longer worry about what I write. I simply write. Because I must. Because I'm suffocating. I write anything. Any way. People can call it what they want: novel, essay, poem, autobiography, testimony, narrative, memory exercise, or nothing at all. I don't even know, myself. Yet what I write feels perfectly familiar to me. No one can say much more than what he has lived.

I'm suffocating. I write whatever crosses my mind. The important thing for me is the exorcism. The liberation of something. Of someone. Of myself perhaps. Deliverance. Catharsis. I'm suffocating. I can see no window in this cellar. And I push against the walls of my asphyxiation with the battering ram of words. If, after all this, the walls still don't come down, surely a passerby will hear the anarchic rush of my language, or the savage SOS of my death throes. I have done enough thinking. People think too much around here. Or maybe no one thinks at all. I'm tired. Now I knock on closed doors. I paw at the ground. I shout. I call out. I scream. Will my cries for help manage to move anyone? To reach some sympathetic target? I don't know. But unhappiness, misery, despair, rage, rivers, storms, blood, fire, seas, hurricanes, my country, trees, mountains, my people, women, children, old men, all men, all things, and all beings swell in my voice, to the point where, should I fail, I'll have been truly alone. Terrifyingly alone. Horribly alone.

I accuse, in advance, the Pharisians of in vitro culture.

Lazy philosophers! Rid yourselves of the bacilli of pure intellect. Explain to me how it is that people all over the world go thirsty. That malnourished peasants feed themselves rock porridge. That children die from fever. That my friend is gone, lost in the American army's invasion of Vietnam. Explain to me that woman who left and never came back. The Third World bullied, ridiculed, despised. The threat of Imperial Powers. The blindness of people who don't know how to decipher the graffiti of time's passing. The illiterate pride of dictators who stomp on the dreams of their people. The shuddering of death. The tremors of life. The sadness of some. The joy of others. The enigma of love. My beating heart. Explain all that to me. I'll always have the patience to listen and to hear – as long as, at the end of it all, there is action.

In the meantime, I speak with the voice of Raynand, with the voice of Paulin, with my own voice. Raynand and Paulin are one and the same character. I am their voice – at times weak, at times strong, but always there. Always present. The voice of the Third World torn apart. The voice suffocated beneath giant shadows. Raynand, tired, tries to find himself in Paulin, an image of the one who fights to transform repugnant realities. And in the interval, one voice remains audible: Raynand's, Paulin's, my own. For myself, I don't know anything about this life that sweeps me up in a set of mirages and enduring utopias.

■   ■   ■

Eleven hours and thirty minutes of night and thick shadows. Raynand has been walking for hours. He's become a pair of legs that walk. Between Presbytère and the cathedral, the large bulb, hanging from the cylindrical streetlamp, is no longer lit.

Perhaps some of the filaments have broken, scorched by the intense electrical heat? Perhaps the eye of the pear-shaped bulb was shattered by a pretty little stone thrown by the delicate hand of some kid who, on the way to school, wanted to test his skill or prove his virtuosity?

Undoubtedly, the little round stone, washed by last night's rain, had piqued the child's curiosity. He'd stooped down. Picked it up. Thrown it in the direction of the bulb. Surprised. Astonished. Eager to tell his class-mates all about his exploit, his good aim.

Tired, heavy-headed, not really knowing where he's going at this time of night, Raynand tells himself that he has always behaved like a child. Irresponsible. Lighthearted. Carefree. Twenty-eight years, and what had he really done? Almost nothing along the path of blind stones. Absolutely nothing in the intermingling of demented winds.

Without any specific objective, he wanders. Covered in sweat. Feeling in his bones the forceps of anxiety. Fever in his gut. Suddenly, his hairs stand on end. Who could be calling to Raynand in this humid night? His nerves, his senses warn him. What chattering birds scream in the night? What evil beasts flap their featherless wings in the corners of the invertebrate town?

Who is calling to Raynand in the tentacled darkness? Jungle of invisible arms. Sharp edges of flattened voices. Viscosity of hairy hands. Forest of vines and glutinous intestines. Piles of ripped-out fingernails. Emaciated faces. His nerves, his senses on high alert.

The call persists in the suffocating heat of the night. Overheating of his intestines. Bursting of his glands. The sky covers the town with a thick, mysterious form. Someone still calls out to Raynand. Could it be a pros-titute in the darkness? No . . . more like the sound of metal-tipped shoes. Frightened, Raynand turns around. He looks around. Turns in circles around himself. Can't make anything out. Can't see anything anymore. He walks a little faster. Who would want to interrupt his peaceful stroll? Someone follows more and more closely on his heels. He crosses Alexandre Pétion Place, just in front of the cathedral. Then, unable to hold back any longer, he takes off as fast as he can toward Bonne-Foi Street. He charges toward Jean-Jacques Dessalines Boulevard, where he hopes to come across some insomniac night owls.

Should he scream? Call for help? His mouth full of saliva. His tongue heavy . . . The breath and the spittle of his pursuers hot on his neck. Their foul breath, like burning vapor, smolders in his ears, dries out his skin. Smell of sulfur. Acidic little bites. Their forked claws are already tearing at his back.

If only he can reach Saint Joseph's Gate in time. There'll be people there. Help. Oh swift feet of my turbulent childhood! Have I ever eaten anything without giving you the biggest share? Have I ever drunk anything without offering you the most delicious portion? Nimble feet, languishing in the sweet, slow music of yesteryear, run faster! If anything happens to me, I shall blame you . . . My mother will be so sorry . . . If I die . . . And my beloved Solange? To never see her again?

It's as if I've lost a piece of myself . . . Oh swift feet of my adolescence! Don't even stop to catch your breath! Sports competitions. Long-distance races. Bitter races. The old high-school courtyard. Vincent Stadium. Sylvio Cator Stadium. Marathon. A rowdy crowd. Bravo for the champion – three laps in three minutes, ten seconds! Unbeatable record . . . Champ de Mars of my teenage years! Fields marked with quicklime. One hundred meters flat. Just let me keep my lead. Reach Saint Joseph's Gate. Get there before them. Safe and sound . . . To once again see the sun shine on my country, on the hills, the rooftops, the streets . . .

Raynand feels them on his heels. Close. Far too close. Stumbling against a piece of broken concrete, he falls down at the intersection of Jean-Jacques Dessalines Boulevard and Fronts-Forts Street. Face-first. He keeps rolling. Then comes to a complete stop. On his back. His body, a blazing torch. His limbs, bursts of flames. His head on fire, a flaming mass filled with exploding shells. Eyes open, he looks at the corner of the street whizzing by like wagons jam-packed together, mounted on rails like a high-speed train, an express train to the sea. It's funny . . . I'm taking the midnight express. It's beautiful, this aboveground landscape of neon signs! The sky chopped into ragged pieces. Neon flowers light up . . . shut off . . . light up again . . . Blue . . . red . . . green . . . yellow. How quickly it goes by, this silent, freewheeling train to the dock! Blue-green . . . blue-red . . . deep yellow. Stereophonic surge in the middle of the night. The street lets out a long trumpet blast between the two rows of sealed-up houses. Brains crushed. Head aflame. Torchlight tattoo. Carnival. Mask. Fear . . . dead silence . . . Is this what it's like to die?

■ ■ ■

Rapid fluttering of eyelids. Little by little, Raynand comes to. He vaguely recognizes the few objects that pass into his line of sight and lash at his memory.

A half dream in which, still blurry, the various things in his little room slowly begin to take shape. His vision floats in the oppressive space. A vast, viscous sea! Each wave turns up innumerable pink fish. Raynand's room looks to him like an immense aquarium filled with blond octopuses wrapped around hundreds of swimming arms. But then in the next second, he sees himself on the edge of a lake. He's skipping stones along the water's surface; the waves send a circular message toward the sandy shore.

From his bed, Raynand looks around confusedly. Looks out from the depths. He tries to bring the contents of the modest room into focus. In the center, four mahogany chairs surrounding a gueridon. In the south corner, a shaky table. Near the open door, a hanging wardrobe propped up against the wall. Seated, arms crossed, a brown-haired chap he doesn't recognize, a stranger. At the foot of his bed, standing, an older woman on whom Raynand's glance rests affectionately.

– Mama Marguerite, I'd like a little water.

– Right away, Raynand.

A minute later, the stranger slowly raises Raynand's head. He takes little sips of the cold water from the glass held to his lips by his mother, wilted, suddenly grown old. Once he has finished drinking, he smiles faintly and looks with curiosity on the stranger seated near his bed.

– And who is this?

– This is Monsieur Paulin. He found you at the intersection of Jean-Jacques Dessalines Boulevard and Fronts-Forts Street yesterday, in terrible shape.

– What?

– He found you stretched out on the ground, unconscious. He was able to get your address and to bring you home in a taxi, thanks to the little notebook you had in the pocket of your shirt.

Raynand, grateful, thanks Paulin by squeezing his hand. After a long silence, in a worried tone, he questions his mother.

– Where is Solange, Mama? Has she not come to see me? Tell me, Mama, does she know. Does Solange know?

. . .

Raynand had met Solange some months earlier at a birthday party at a friend's house. From the moment they met, he'd been struck by the captivating gaze of this girl with summer in her eyes, spring in her smile. Irresistible magic spell of a tropical princess who wears the two great seasons of the Caribbean islands on her face. At first he'd thought it was merely a physical attraction and that he'd never really get caught up in such an affair. But love planted its hooks in him. Deeply. Indelible tattoo.

On their first date he realized that any attempt to fight that feeling of love at first sight would have been in vain; all resistance futile; any effort to escape the viselike grip of fate could only fail. So he spoke with her at length about his feelings. Seated on marble chairs at Pigeon Place, they chatted, at a distance from all passersby.

– I've thought of you constantly, Solange.

– Me too, I've been thinking of you.

– Ever since we met, I've been caught up in a whirl of dizzying thoughts and crazy obsessions. On the very first night I saw you, I was turned inside out by your gaze. Where do you live, Solange?

– Saint Antoine district.

– I'll come see you.

– No, you mustn't come. My home is like a prison. My father, a tyrant. And my mother can do nothing about it. No, you mustn't come.

– I understand, I suppose. We're all trapped in a dark well, heads thrown back, bodies sucked violently toward a bottomless abyss.

– Raynand, I trust you.

Deeply troubled, Solange stood up suddenly. With a trembling voice, she tried to explain why she couldn't stay out much longer. Raynand took her hand for a moment and said to her shyly:

– I'm crazy, truly crazy about you. What more can I tell you, now that I bear what feels like a centuries-old love for you?

– Don't say anything more.

– When can we see one another again?

– I don't know.

Solange begged Raynand to let her leave and walked away pensively. She crossed the road, visibly unnerved by Raynand's persistent stare piercing the nape of her neck and her spine with strange little pricks.

■　■　■

A week later, they were supposed to see one another again at the Bicentennial, the same spot. Raynand had been waiting there for half an hour, thinking to himself that his own heart had conspired against him. He smoked incessantly. Looked every which way. If only Solange would get there already! Of course, she'll come . . . The world has revolved a million times on its axis. And each morning the sun rises again . . . She'll come. Every rib of our sensual, hysterical planet has shuddered. Yet with each dawn, a fresh breeze gives the plants a brand-new hairdo. She'll come, I just know it. She'll come . . .

Seeing Solange arrive from the other corner of Exposition Boulevard nearly took his breath away. Nervously, she came to sit down. Raynand could feel the heat of her body. Pressed against one another for a long while, they forgot there was any such thing as time, as things, as the sound of waves crashing against the jetty, as the passerby who looked at them oddly. They didn't even notice that the stars had disappeared and that menacing clouds had begun to darken the sky through the cracks between the streaks of rain. The first drops brought them back to the reality of the outside world. They had just enough time to cross the street and hail a taxi, which brought them first to Solange's house, giving Raynand the opportunity to discover where she lived.

The next day, at six in the evening, Raynand was in the Saint Antoine area, prowling around Solange's house, hoping to catch sight of her.

He came. He went. He lay in wait. Not even thinking about the fact that people in the neighborhood might take him for a suspicious character, a burglar even . . . taking careful stock of the surroundings in preparation for a potential heist. What must they be imagining, her neighbors? Merely that I'm a bit odd . . . A madman . . . Well, yes, I'm crazy about her. Ah! Her house! The iron gate is open. There's a tree in the courtyard. Branches. Leaves. Light. No, that's not her home. I alone am her home. I breathe her in. She is in me. If only I could go inside for a moment. See her. Speak to her . . .

– Is anyone there?

And just like that Raynand found himself knocking timidly on the entryway door that opened onto the brick-paved gallery. A young girl came to let him in, invited him to take a seat in the salon, and went to let Solange's mother know of his visit.

Raynand took a quick glance around the room. Nestled himself into an overstuffed chair placed right in front of a rectangular mirror hanging on the wall. Like that he'd be able to look at himself from time to time. To keep an eye on his posture. To monitor his gestures. His psychology professor, speaking on the subject of behaviorism, had said that one's body language could give away certain psychological secrets. He looked at himself in the mirror. I'm not too bad-looking with my square forehead and thick eyebrows. But I'd look better with a little tuft of hair. It seems my left eye is smaller than the right one. I have a wide nose, flattened at the base, with gaping nostrils that look like they belong on an ox. Dear God! Is it possible I'm a little bit ugly? Could I be unpleasant to look at? Solange's parents seem so well-off. The most elegant house in the neighborhood . . . A lovely salon. A television set. A stereo. I'll move in here. I'll stay here. A rolling stone gathers no moss. I'll live with my in-laws. Ha! There they are now.

– Good evening, young man.

– Good evening.

Solange's mother, a young woman, and her husband, slightly older, take a seat on the sofa to Raynand's right.

– I'm Monsieur Raynand.

– Aha! Lovely. Solange has told us about you.

– Really?

– We've made you wait. Please excuse us.

– Oh, no, not at all! I should be the one apologizing. I should have let you know I'd be visiting . . . Well, I mean . . . I should have warned you. Terribly gauche of me.

– Never mind all that, Monsieur Raynand, it's no matter. On the contrary, we're very happy you've come to visit.

– Well, then, thank you.

– Solange has spoken of you in such flattering terms that we've been quite keen to meet you.

– I certainly hope she hasn't overstated things!

– I don't believe she's overstated anything, or that she's made any mistake, Monsieur Raynand.

Rosie, Solange's mother, had excused herself from the room. Meanwhile, the two men had begun a meandering conversation, going over various current events. It was a veritable duel of information in which, out of fatuousness and pedantry on both sides, the most sophisticated expressions, the most unusual words, scholarly terms, Latin citations, newspaper columns, film titles, actors' names trampled any common sense, destroyed basic reason. Raynand understood from the outset that this was a fencing match of which the only honorable outcome could be complete and total victory over his adversary. The salon was immediately transformed into a veritable arena where farcical gladiators faced off against one another in the winds of hollow phrases. A fight between cocks armed with fake spurs. Unfortunately for Raynand, he wasn't a mere spectator. He was the one doing battle in the middle of the amphitheater. A 100-watt lightbulb over his skull. He was sweating. The sweat was running down his temples in rapid little streams. Naturally, Vietnam was high on the list of topics. The devaluation of the British pound put Great Britain in a delicate position and ultimately gave rise to an idiotic analysis of the ravages of inflation and the fragility of the American dollar. Third World countries should stake it all on the hostility between the two major political blocks and just move back and forth between capitalism and socialism, a third way thus opening like a new canal called on to link extreme poles and reconcile the major ideologies of the twentieth century. Doctor Christiaan Barnard in South Africa had successfully performed a sensational heart transplant. Russian and American rockets had landed on the moon. The verbal battle raged on between Raynand and Solange's father. The attacks and the feints multiplied. Raynand was sweating. The sweat pooled in little beads on his forehead. He blotted his face elegantly while looking at himself in the mirror.

Rosie had returned with a tray bearing three small cocktail glasses. Raynand was served first. He immediately began sipping the sweet-smelling pink liquid, pretending to find it delightful, whereas he would have much preferred a nice glass of rum. He courageously withstood the sugary drink, which wasn't easy, given that his palate, if it could be called that, was accustomed to stiffer stuff. He took longer than necessary to finish his drink. He had to take advantage of the unexpected pause. He knew full well the terms of engagement, the detours, the traps, the infernal itinerary of this exhausting intellectual adventure. And where it was all leading. The assaults would become even more violent. The key questions hadn't yet been touched upon. But he had to triumph, whatever the cost,

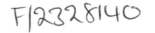

or at the very least manage a tie. He had a feeling the hits were going to keep coming. Even after a half hour of dialogue, the look in his adversary's eyes was by no means comforting. Thus he didn't dare ask after Solange. He had to be a good sport, hide his weaknesses, trust his own armor, he said to himself. He's already in the ring. He's got to pick up the challenge. Suddenly, the gong broke the silence. Round two. The enemy harassed him with questions at once pertinent and skillful. Driven back either against the ropes or into a corner, on some diagonal without exit, Raynand was determined to answer blow for blow, even if he had to transgress all rules of fair play, all rules of chivalry. He wouldn't even consider giving up. Never. He had to win. Solange's father put down his empty glass and leaned in closer to his interlocutor.

– Monsieur Raynand, I'm told you're studying law and economics.

– Yes, I'm in my third year.

– You must have quite a lot of work, in addition to your daily activities.

– Work overwhelms us, overburdens us. We're overloaded with tasks to accomplish. But that's life. We rest only when we're dead.

– When all's said and done, that's certainly to be preferred. One has to prepare one's future while one is young, I'd say. Do you work all day, Monsieur Raynand?

– No. Only in the morning. I teach social science in a high school. And I teach literature courses at several secondary schools.

– Once you've completed your university studies, do you intend to remain in the country?

– Oh, no! I plan to head for Canada, where I expect to get a work contract. A friend up there has begun the process; he assures me that I'll easily be making two thousand dollars a month.

– I certainly agree with that plan. I encourage you to keep moving in that direction.

Raynand was sure to have won the battle, having unloaded a whole host of lies and counterfeit currency on his adversary. He felt uncomfortable – ashamed, even. He had been diminished in his own esteem. He had fought with forbidden arms. A combat without glory. A false victory. A face-off between clowns in a circus that one leaves disillusioned. Sweat on his temples. His skull under a burning, blinding 100-watt lightbulb.

Suddenly, he got up to leave. He had the urge to let out a full-throated laugh. To laugh to exhaustion, till he had no more breath left in him. To scream. To yell. To explode. To burst into a thousand tiny pieces of flesh. To become a blood spatter, a flattened mass, crushed under one of those caterpillar tanks. He held out his hand to his hosts and asked them to pass his good wishes to Solange. She was on the second floor. She came lightly down the stairs, entered the salon, and, visibly intimidated, greeted her friend just as he was being accompanied to the little iron gate.

Raynand walked quickly. He wanted to see a familiar face as soon as possible. He wanted to speak to someone close to him. To tell the truth. To get rid of the vile and alienating straitjacket weighing on his shoulders. Scrape off the mud of imposture. He quickened his pace. He was almost tempted to run. He smoked, biting on his lip each time he took a puff. Yes, he needed to tell the truth. To speak to a friend. To shout from every street corner, I'm not a student, not a professor of anything, and I have no travel plans in sight. But they're the ones who wanted all those lies. Had I confessed that I'm constantly unemployed, they wouldn't have given me the time of day. But they sure did smile when I told them about my plan to go abroad and about the two thousand dollars I'd be getting in Canada. The old fool twirled his mustache and gave me a sidelong glance, seemed pretty satisfied.

When Raynand got close to his house, he charged into the home of a neighbor, a childhood friend.

Once there, he burst out laughing, to the stupefaction of the people there, who had no idea what to make of his strange behavior. He was laughing like a madman. Clutching his stomach. Undoing his belt. He threw himself onto the narrow iron bed. Rolled around on the mattress. Fell to the ground.

Raynand stood up and kept on laughing. He woke up the kids, who'd already gone to bed. No one was able to interpret this prolonged fit of laughter, interspersed with giggles. A few minutes later, his laugh changed strangely into a combination of staccato gasps and guttural spasms. His chest convulsed. It was as if he were suffocating in a spacesuit. Or rather in some kind of steel diving gear. Asphyxiating in a space filled with octopuses that tightened their grip around his torso. Lungs trapped in an iron straitjacket. Then he began to weep, to cry like a child, without ever getting a chance – or the guts – to tell anyone how it was that he'd discovered, through painful experience, that his mind was sick, his heart unstable, and his spirit deranged by a state of near-schizophrenic alienation.

. . .

In the very beginning, Raynand visited Solange twice a week. Once fully welcomed into the household, hardly a day went by where he didn't see her. Their love seemed to get stronger in the relative freedom they had to spend time together, in the little routine they'd created, the gestures, the words, the shared debauchery – that is to say, all the ritual that comes with the early days of a love story. Each time they made love was marked by rich ceremony, for which Raynand proved himself a passionate and talented officiant. Strange liturgy of kisses, ticklings, caresses, nibblings, and acrobatic hip movements in their horizontal altercations. And Raynand became an ever more fervent believer during these solemn and sensual sexual high masses. He celebrated his passion in a feverish language that demanded no artifice, because – for once – he was truly sincere.

– Solange, I lived so many crippled romances that my heart came out of it all somehow unhinged, used up. Then I met you. And now today, like a child without any memories, I say yes to love – to you, whom I love. I'm happy.

– I haven't any doubt about that. I'm happy, too.

– Solange, I need you to love me without hesitation, I need you to trust me.

– I love you and I trust you, my dearest.

– Ah! Do you have any idea what a slave I am to your charms? Even in my own home, I remain your slave. All the most familiar objects in my room are marked by your name, your face, your presence. Night and day, you dance in my head. Ever since I met you, I'm nothing more than a home for you. Besieged from all directions by your image, I've come to know the full extent of love's tyranny.

Solange stretched out naked. And Raynand caressed her face and belly with his hands.

– You're so beautiful, Solange. Nature could lose her bloom, the wind of death could blow cold over all things, day and night play hide-and-go-seek in a ballet of light and shadow, you'd remain the most delicate, the most beautiful.

– I love you, Raynand. I belong to you. I'll always be yours. You know how happy I am with you. But great joy is just like great sorrow. I don't sleep at night. You slip into my room on the wings of silence. You enter me. Your presence stands guard over me.

– You too, my love, you move through me. I don't sleep at night either. You walk in my room. You unmake my bed; you make it back up. Without making a sound, you cover me with your gaze. You become the air I breathe. I raise my eyes, you're there on the ceiling. Entirely encircled, I raise high the white flag of surrender. I am your slave.

– I'll grant you no quarter, my love – no peace – in love. I am your mistress.

– I kiss your feet like no other. I place my heart in your hands. I beg you, don't break it, Solange – it already hurts so much. It's up to you whether I end up a wise man or a fool. Save me by cradling our love. You are the green light on my entire life. You can make of me your spouse or a lowly wanderer.

– But, Raynand, I love you, I adore you, what could you possibly fear? Is it doubt about my feelings that makes you go on endlessly like this?

– No, it has nothing to do with doubting you. My worries come from a much deeper unease. In my experience, love has always been an explosive mixture. But I'm always the one who gets torn apart, left in pieces. And life is just one hassle after the next. On top of that, misery seems always to be knocking at the doors of the living. And so many trials . . . At the tiniest spark, I explode and am irreparably destroyed.

– But, Raynand, do you think our love so fragile that it wouldn't be able to face such challenges? Don't you know I've placed my love for you above all pride, above all modesty?

– I know, Solange.

– So then why must you speak this way? Our love isn't a fire, built on twigs, that the slightest wind can extinguish.

– Yes, I know that.

Raynand let his hands wander over Solange's breasts, causing them to tremble more and more.

– Raynand, take me now. I want you to take me. I can't stand it any longer. Sweetheart, my darling, take me. I'm your puppy dog. Your sweet little puppy dog.

– Solange, my angel, I'm the one who's your puppy dog. Your faithful lapdog.

And with that, Raynand seized her in his arms. Encircled the excited panther her body had become. The vertigo of his mouth took over. The softness of her skin. The perfume of her neck. The breath of her heaving chest. He penetrated her slowly, voluptuously, in the soft, moist depths of her infinite flesh. She quivered and released a deep sigh, punctuated by little cries and lascivious moans. Two dogs in heat embarked on the unbridled coitus of love and death, they glimpsed a flash of eternity, the divine shimmerings of ecstasy.

≈ ≈ ≈

Raynand spent several months living only for love, until the day he began to detect slight changes in Solange's words and overall attitude toward him. From then on, he became consumed with worry, tortured by anxiety. Solange's parents were less solicitous. He went to her house several times in a row without finding her at home. He began to have doubts, to picture . . . His imagination went over every possible explanation. His doubts became painful certainty, an intolerable torture, one Saturday night when he saw Solange emerge from the car of a certain Gaston, a regular at the house for the past couple of months. Raynand refused nonetheless to let himself sink fully into the quicksand of infernal jealousy. He gathered all his courage and forced himself that very night to speak to Solange without even mentioning Gaston – with his air of a self-satisfied pig, a true barbarian, powerful and arrogant. Raynand was so desperate to hold on to his love, his main reason for living, that he chose a more subtle strategy.

– Solange, why has making love become a desert, a loneliness, a barrier, a distancing – when it should be bringing us closer together? Why this exile? Why have I been cast away into this painful absence of you? I'm suffering terribly. I look for you, you run from me, you're moving further and further away from me. Tell me, Solange, is the island so far away that it can only be reached with eyes closed, in the infinite rush of a dream? Such that upon waking, eyes opened, the very image disappears? You are a shadow that obsesses me, killing me slowly in the dusty mirror of my fantasies.

– But, Raynand, I'm right here, next to you.

– You don't understand, Solange, For the past week I've come every evening and never found you at home. Because of you, sadness has enveloped me beneath her gray wing. My obsession, my misery – they circulate in my blood, clothed in your gaze. The wound of absence. How old is our love, that it has me so afraid of losing you? My heart already counts up to a thousand tremblings and still hasn't finished. Is it possible that before I even met you, you were the sovereign ruler over the kingdom of my life – is this why I'm so weak, so vulnerable, so pitifully prostrate at your feet?

– Raynand, it's like you're insulting me. If you're speaking to me like this it's because you don't trust me. What are you accusing me of exactly?

– Solange, why haven't I been able to see you? For a week now it's been like a conspiracy. I come here and you're never home. I can't take it anymore. My head hurts so badly. I'm suffering body and soul. You laid my heart in your lap, you undressed it. And now I'm completely naked. Nothing more than a wretched stray dog.

Solange moves closer to Raynand on the living room couch. She gives him a light kiss below the ear, making him feel as if some sensual and exciting little creature had just kissed his neck. Raynand stared at her, a rod of doubt planted right between his eyes, just above his nose. Solange dropped her head. They talked for more than a half hour. Kissed passionately. And left each other at about nine that evening. As always, Solange brought Raynand to the little green wrought-iron gate and said: See you tomorrow, my love, my tender lapdog!

That was their last *tête-à-tête*.

Raynand had no inkling that such a disaster was coming. Nevertheless, the following Sunday, through the open front door, he saw Solange in Gaston's arms.

It was a violent shock. A sudden gust of wind. A cyclone. His head jerked back. He almost lost his footing. Out of modesty, he made sure he wasn't noticed. He'd have felt ridiculous. Like a lapdog, tail tucked between his legs, he went away, all his limbs trembling. His skin felt like it had been overcome with a sudden fever, intense and profound. His stomach churned. His intestines writhed like a snake hit in the head with a rock. No, like an earthworm wound around itself, its head crushed under someone's heel, every ring broken. I'm enveloped in shadows. The night is more present deep inside of me than anywhere else . . . than under the spherical cap deprived of sunlight . . . than in all things cut off from the light. I'm irrevocably draped in darkness under the sordid weight of an endless night. The beast is neither dead nor vanquished. It lies within me. Of one body with my nerves and my vertebrae. I am pity incarnate, misery itself. A pathetic human being. A sadness without greatness. The infected wound of a dog without a master. Just trample me, Solange. Spit on me. Crush me like an insect. Crush my worm's head. Love turns bitter in my hands. It burns me with a voracious flame. It is without pity. It nibbles at my entrails, killing me slowly but surely. Assassinating me. It strangles me mercilessly. It's the queen bee who, in a whirlwind, kills any male who comes near her. It's the female hippopotamus who kills her partner on the bottom of the ocean while mating. My Solange! It isn't her fault. It's my fault entirely. I had the audacity to love her. I ventured into a no-man's-land. And not by accident. But because I simply could not do otherwise. And so it is that now even retreat is painful. All I leave behind are strips of flesh caught on the teeth of barbed wire.

Raynand walked for hours without even realizing it. He was really just walking in circles, looping endlessly around the same block of houses next to Saint Antoine. He'd become a pair of walking legs in the wind, heading nowhere. He had the vague sense of being followed. He took off running. He ran without knowing where he was headed. At one point he felt like an invisible giant crane had lifted him up and flung him toward the stars. Having fallen back down to earth, he was seized yet again by clusters of invisible hands, irresistibly powerful – brutally restrained by long, sharpened claws skinning him alive. He lost all sense of space, of time, of the surrounding world, of himself even.

When he came to he found himself in his bedroom. Stretched out in his own bed. His head heavy. Bruises on his arms. He tried to sit up. His body, worked over by a cement truck, remained immobile. His mother, drained of color, sat at the foot of the bed. A grave-faced stranger was seated, arms crossed, just next to the door.

His mother informs him that the stranger is Paulin, the generous passerby who'd found him unconscious at the intersection of Jean-Jacques Dessalines Boulevard and Fronts-Forts Street.

Paulin came to see Raynand through the whole time of his recovery, becoming his dearest friend.

■   ■   ■

As a child, on Sunday mornings, I often saw my mother using a wood-handled knife to slit the neck of a chicken or a rooster right through to the throat (the jugular, she'd say). Coming back from the seven o'clock mass at the Petit Séminaire, it was always a treat for me to be present for – to participate passionately and feverishly in – the preparations for this good old-fashioned Creole cuisine. The bloody feast of flesh crackling in the pale yellow oil of the saucepan. Perfectly content to be a part of this culinary ritual, I helped my mother make the fire. I followed all of her instructions meticulously. I heated the water we used to parboil the chicken. I danced with joy at the moment when, mortally wounded, the bird did a frenzied farewell casser-banda. * *Desperate beating of wings. I didn't realize that the innocent beast was actually suffering. I only knew that three hours later, the time it would take to cook and serve it, I'd be eating grilled flesh, a delicious morsel of roasted chicken the color of burnt mahogany.*

* A rhythmic dance style associated with the *Gède nanchon* in vodou ceremonies.

Back then I had a neighborhood friend who brought me a packet of sugar pilfered from his aunt's boutique every night. He was often beaten for failing to memorize his catechism lesson or for not doing his math homework. The bastard son of a white man passing through the region, he had straight hair and blue eyes. He lived as the quintessential pariah in the community. And he was usually addressed by the pejorative nickname "wicked manioc-eating white boy." As for me, I never picked on him. Time and again, in fact, during any number of full-blown fistfights and ferocious hand-to-hand combats, I smashed in the face of whatever troublemakers had gone after him for no reason. Things went on like that for two years, which seems like an eternity to me today. Battling the same little adversaries. United in the same turmoil. Divvying up the booty from our petty thefts. Playing hooky together. And, above all, hating that toothless old aunt who all too often struck my friend with a bull pizzle.

This went on until the day he caught a bad flu, having gone out in the rain to run an errand for that miserable aunt. He didn't last long. He died one afternoon in May, the month of beautiful flowers. Or at least that's what I heard people saying that afternoon. I was on my way home from school. But I didn't yet understand the truly tragic and macabre nature of death. It was only the following day that I came face-to-face with the brutal reality of this separation, when my mother made me put on my white suit – to accompany my friend on a long trip, she said. His final journey. At the cemetery, the coffin was placed next to a deep, freshly dug hole in the ground. When the cover of the casket was lifted so that we could take one last look at the embalmed little cadaver, the toothless old aunt started whimpering, morbid and inconsolable. And there I saw my innocent childhood companion laid out. His eyes open. Like those of a fish. Apparently, it had been impossible to close his eyelids, stiffened by the cold of the morgue. People let loose piercing cries. But me, I looked into his open bluish eyes. Fish eyes. Unmoving. And I understood right away that death is a deep sleep with eyes wide open. A dream perhaps. A dream with no awakening.

It was a horrific shock for me when, using a series of interwoven ropes, they slipped the tiny closed coffin – gloomily nailed shut, hermetically sealed – into the dark ditch and began covering it with quickly thrown handfuls of brown earth. My blood turned to ice in my veins. Tears ran into my mouth. A taste of salt mixed with mucus. It was then that I felt the pain of ultimate separation. But when I think about it today, I still can't bring myself to forgive that old aunt for taking away my first friend and for having poisoned – with the whip, with insults, with mistreatment – the short life of a kid who was no worse than any other. An innocent who never got the chance to count ten, twelve, fifteen, twenty years alongside me. To live other joys. Other sorrows. Other pain. All that he would have lived with those blue eyes of his. Open like those of a fish.

■ ■ ■

Ah! My son! sighs old Marguerite, thinking of Raynand. From the first cry of infancy, we mothers are never again fully alive. The child leaves our body and takes with it a part of us that we can never reclaim but that we're forever attached to, that we're forever drawn to despite ourselves. The split between mother and son is only superficial. If the child is hurt, it is our own flesh that bleeds. If he takes risks, our hair stands on end and anguish rips apart our entrails. If he suffers from the smallest thing, we cry our eyes out to the very last tear. If he dies, we shut down completely, trapped despairingly in an infernal interior prison. The terrible suffering of the snake that bites its own tail. Should senseless people see fit to crack open our hearts, split open our bellies, they'll still find there the bed of love where the child once slept, always freshly made. The umbilical cord never breaks between mother and child. There is no blade capable of cutting the ties that bind the two . . .

Marguerite is brought out of these reflections by the arrival of a stranger.

She gets up from her low chair. Places the coffee grinder on the white wood table.

She moves toward the stranger, wiping her hands on her calico skirt.

– Hello, Madame, says the stranger, brusquely.

– Hello, Sir, responds Marguerite, nervously.

– Are you Raynand's mother?

– Yes, Raynand is my son. Did you need him for something?

– I'd like to speak with him, yes.

– Raynand has been out for a while now. He'll surely be back in a moment or two. Would you like to wait for him?

– No, that won't be necessary, responds the gentleman, annoyed.

– What was it you wanted to speak to him about? You might leave him a message, even a word or two.

– That wouldn't be the same thing, no. Nevertheless, continues the stranger, tensely emphasizing each word, I'll ask you to let him know that Gaston – Gaston, in person – came to see him. He'll understand what that means. If he isn't crazy, he'll understand very well.

– But what's going on? What has he done to you? I'm his mother – certainly I have the right to know. Monsieur Gaston, please tell me.

– Well, all right! Tell him to stop hanging around Solange. Around her house. Tell him he isn't wanted. That if this continues he'll have real worries. Big problems. It's a short trip from stubbornness and imprudence to death. So tell him he should be careful not to go stomping around in my garden.

Gaston departs angrily. Appalled, hand to her chin, Marguerite doesn't know what to think. She had already told Raynand to let go of this thing with Solange. This old love story. And now things were getting complicated. Completely stupefied, dragging her feet in their leather slippers, she goes back to her coffee grinder. The bag empty, she crumples into the low chair. Anxious. Anguished. Raynand must leave – it's the only solution. He must leave and make his life elsewhere, before his roots push any deeper into this cruel soil, before his branches become prisoner of this mess of vines that will only drink up his sap and make of him a pile of dried-out fibers! Ah! My child, a green tree that hasn't even borne fruit as yet! Why? Why do they want to strip from me my nine months of torment? My painful pregnancy. The pain of my sleepless night at the hospital. Childbirth. The profound tearing. The sharp ripping of my belly. The twisting of my guts. Painful pushing forward of life. Who would steal from me my eleven months of breast-feeding? All the clothes washing. My patience. My tears. My hopes. All those dreams that are exactly as old as my child.

– So, Mama, have you finished grinding the coffee? says Raynand, coming through the door.

– Not yet, darling, responds Marguerite in a voice marked with melancholy tenderness.

– But what's wrong, Mama? You seem like you've been crying. What happened while I was gone?

– Somebody named Gaston came to see you. He was furious and made threats against you. It has something to do with Solange.

– So that's it, then – we aren't free? Since when can't a person go for a walk, wander around?

– Try to understand, my darling. You're not yet even fully recovered. You're still ill. And I'm just sick about it. It wasn't long ago that I nearly died of shock when Paulin brought you here, bones broken, face swollen with bruises.

– But, Mama, I haven't done anything wrong. They're the ones persecuting me, as if my very presence is an annoyance.

– Clearly that's the case. Your presence has become intolerable. The only solution is to leave, especially seeing as you're not really doing much of anything here.

– So you want me to leave, Mama?

– Yes, my son. You'll never have the upper hand with them. I'm old – there's nothing left of me but skin and bones. I wouldn't even make a good mouthful. They want a nice healthy, muscular body. Get out of here – as far away as you can.

– You're asking me to run away, Mama. To give in like a coward to the scare tactics of some good-for-nothing.

– Think about it, my son. I'm speaking from experience and from my heart. I only want what's best for you. Listen to me. Leave, my child. These are not idle threats. Gaston has connections in the government; he's a known killer. I'm begging you, Raynand. Leave immediately.

– Fine . . . let's say I accept. How would we manage the trip?

– I'll go see our neighbor, captain of LA GRÂCE DE DIEU – the one who traffics between the islands. We'll work something out for the costs. You'll go to Nassau. You'll find work there. You'll make a lot of money. After a while, you could maybe even go on to New York.

– So you're set on me leaving forever?

– The years run by like water, my darling. This is the time to think of your future, you'll see.

Shirtless, wearing only a pair of underpants, torn at the crotch, Raynand listens carefully to his mother. For the first time, he seems to take the old woman's suggestions seriously.

– Tell me, Mama, won't you be sad living all alone?

– Of course, I'll be sad in the beginning. But I'll manage. I'm agreeing to this little sacrifice for you. For both of us. For both our happiness. For your safety.

– You still haven't told me how we'll manage this.

– I'll go talk to Murat, the captain, this very night. He won't refuse me this favor. It's his job to bring Haitians to Nassau.

– But, Mama, we don't have any money. A trip like this is expensive. We don't even have enough money to pay for food or the rent.

– Let me handle it, my dear. There's no other solution for the moment. All the young people in the neighborhood are doing the same thing. Don't stay here. Go – and forget Solange. Forget Gaston and all the other cannibals who eat the flesh of our children, who chew up their bones. Go far away from these people who rip apart mothers' guts, trample women's hearts, and devour the best young growth in the fields we've been cultivating endlessly.

– I understand what you're saying, Mama. I accept it. You can go ahead and speak to Captain Murat.

– I'll make sure you get out of here as soon as possible. In Nassau you can sort out your papers to establish residency in New York. It's much easier over there. Don't stay and waste away here. The Caribbean gods will open the way for you, my son.

His vision wearied by the room's low ceiling, Raynand listens attentively to his mother's words. Then he lets his mind wander. Numbed by the overwhelming summer heat. Heavy headed. His gaze follows the buzzing, staccato flight of an enormous fly. A screwworm fly . . . that's a sign of good luck and of bounty; a sign of wealth to come. This age we're living in is made for traveling. In tenth grade, the literature professor often said that any intellectual worth his salt had to travel . . . See the wide world . . . New York Harbor . . . the Eiffel Tower . . . Spit into the Seine . . . Piss in the Saint Laurence . . . See other faces . . . Open his body to all the winds of the universe . . . And his heart to the many faces of love.

– Mama, I'm set on leaving. As you wish. I'll go.

– Thank you, Raynand. I knew you'd understand. Thank you, my darling.

■ ■ ■

I was ten years old when I began to appreciate the power and the omnipresence of money. At all times. In all places. In all things. In the things I loved the most. In things I'd believed were nature's offerings to man. It made me sick. I couldn't accept the nauseating and revolting idea that everything can be bought or sold, depending where you stand. If ever I'd even looked for the border – the dividing line – between buyers and sellers, I wouldn't have been able to find it. With a pang of anguish, I faced the fact that you have to have money to taste such things as candies and fruit. Reluctantly, at the beginning of every month, I handed over wads of dollar bills to the potbellied bursar at Saint-Martial High School. A red-nosed priest who stank of garlic. Who, clearing his throat, used to receive me while seated behind his big desk. Who smelled like bad wine. Who counted my poor mother's money, three wrinkles in his forehead. Whom I loathed for kicking me out of school. Twice. Because my monthly bill hadn't been paid, he made sure to explain.

My bitterness was even greater when I realized that I also needed money to be treated by a doctor. To acquire a much-needed pair of shoes. Or in order for Santa Claus to come. Moreover, I was enraged by all these privations. Source of my first revolts against the adult world. My rage against the system. My refusal to obey laws I didn't understand. My taking a stand against social injustice. My dissidence. My revenge. I resolved to protest in every way. The one who had to deal most often with my bad behavior and my rebellions was Uncle Bernard. Owner of a big boutique, he was the Croesus of the family. Exceptionally stingy, he never forgave a cent of debt among family members. He hated the poor. His heart was made of neither flesh nor wood. For the flesh is weak, and wood heats up when it burns. Truth was, he had no heart. Completely ungenerous. He loved no one. He was harsh. Inflexible with everyone. Cruel. Indifferent to human suffering to the point where he'd refuse to offer the slightest help to my despairing mother, overwhelmed by the weight of her poverty. One day when we had nothing to put on the fire, we went to him, only to be treated like vile parasites. In front of people we didn't even know. That's when I decided to act in my own best interest. I initiated a veritable impoverishment campaign against him, stealing whatever I could from him . . . I went to his grocery store more frequently just so as to advance my plan for meting out justice. Not a day went by that I didn't pilfer some can of something or other, or some money even. My lifestyle improved. I drank milk three times a day. At night I started smoking cigarettes in the toilets. As time went on, I increased my take to up to ten dollars a day, money I spent recklessly with boys from the neighborhood.

One morning when, as usual, I showed up at Uncle Bernard's, I found the living room crowded with strangely dressed people. One of them was wearing a red coat and reading from a Bible with a black cover. I learned from Anna, the servant girl, that this was a Freemason ceremony. A spiritual event. A mystical happening. They'd come as a show of support for their brother-in-arms, victim of inexplicable thefts that had been occurring on a daily basis. They'd come to perform an exorcism of the haunted boutique. To chase away the thieving demon. I also learned that my uncle's wife, for her part, had gone to see several Vodou priests and had just been given the magic recipe that would enable her to catch the thief. People were even predicting that the thief would be dead in less than three days, either when the clock struck twelve noon or at midnight. I stayed till the end of the ceremony, which ended at about eleven in the morning. That afternoon, before the sun had even finished setting, I'd already pilfered a twenty-dollar bill from my uncle's cash register. And I went on messing with him for years. When I finally stopped stealing money from him – a purely personal decision – he died three days later. On a Saturday, at around noon. Result of a brain aneurysm, said the family doctor. His wife followed him to the grave that same year.

The rumor circulated for a long time that his wife had poisoned him, having been unfaithful to him throughout their entire marriage. Her most recent lover was none other than one of the Freemasons, the one who'd played the role of priest the day of that famous exorcism ceremony. That crafty profiteer is still alive. Every time I pass him in the street I can't help but curse his hypocrisy. Yet I pray he lives as long as possible. Certain that he'll leave this world before me to rejoin his mistress in hell.

When I think of this macabre story from so long ago, I always imagine a theater piece with three actors: the adulterous wife, the cuckolded husband, the fraudulent lover. In the wings there's me, hooligan of a nephew, brilliant director of the play "The Other Side of Magic."

■   ■   ■

The bus races along. Raynand is seated nonchalantly in the last row. The back of his head leaning against the window. Fingers trembling nervously. Every so often he shivers lightly. He gets up every morning, goes to his job, his skin slightly feverish. His workplace, a tomato and onion cannery, is twenty minutes away from where he lives – or rather, where he's being hidden by a fellow migrant, a prostitute he'd known once upon a time at a whorehouse on Carrefour Street. Not having a resident's visa, he only goes out to work. Other than that, obliged to stay clear of the police dragnets, he lives holed up in the room offered to him by this kindly woman.

In the month since he's been in Nassau, he's been living on the edge. A real test of his nerves. He knows an immigration agent could catch him at any moment. A fresh hell in a foreign land, in a town he barely knows. Exhausted. Out of his element. Without any roots. His nostrils irritated by the acidic smell of the onions processed in the factory. Respiratory passages blocked, the worst kind of suffering for me. And then there's Mama Marguerite – so far away. She would have fixed me up some refreshing cure. Something with magnesium in it. And some finger biscuit tea. But here I am, with no choice but to take care of this awful flu myself. How I hate having a cold. The snoring. The chewing. The sound of ice cubes and dry crackers in my mouth. The glug-glug I make when I swallow. The vomiting. The farting. The belching. The defecating. The whole digestive ritual. Shameful alimentary liturgy of all human beings. Waste scoria diarrheic shits. Filthy vomit and poo. From the lowliest porter to the most glorious leader of men. A strange folklore passed down from the oldest generations. Fecal ritual left behind by a population of fossils, unsparing of the most beautiful women and the greatest dignitaries on the planet. Someone should erect a universal totem somewhere, and all creatures could gather at its feet, pawing at an immense sea of excrement and urine! Man pretends to be enlightened, though he's nothing more than a charlatan. He thinks he's impressing all the other species with those magic tricks he calls the conquest of the civilized . . . Electricity. Mechanics. Architecture. Ballistics. And from end to end, the tragicomedy of History. Vast circus of dwarves and clowns. An insomniac theater ruled by a guilty conscience. Science, technology, literature, art, politics, war. The fascinating exhibitionism of idiotic spectators, often amnesiac. Smugness in sterile solitude. Solemn masturbation. Buildings and streets, veritable con game, collective falsehood. A network of traps. Every block a multidrawer vault in which the selfish, gathered together as families, close themselves up in the false security of domesticity, really nothing more than the hermeticism of cemeteries. Closed rooms, shantytowns, skyscrapers, hospitals, madhouses, barracks, banks, prisons, factories, churches, museums, stores, castles, palaces, boutiques, warehouses for rockets and bombs – let it all crumble, collapse on itself, melt in an inextinguishable blaze! Ah! Something really isn't right . . . Could I be the only one to see that? How the embers of hell burn my brain! Expiation . . . The supreme punishment . . .

– Hey! Stop! Stop! cries Raynand, having nearly missed the turn where he has to get off to go to the factory.

Raynand pushes the door open, hops down to the sidewalk, watches the bus pull away before crossing the road. At almost the same instant, he's approached by a brawny police officer holding a strapping, menacing dog, its drooling tongue hanging out of its mouth like a wide, fleshy leaf. Not understanding English, much less the question being posed to him by the officer, but guessing at a word or two here and there (words like: refugee, illegal, unwanted, travel, passport), Raynand turns on his heel to get away from the policeman. He only gets the chance to take a single step. With a ferocious leap, the guard dog grabs him by the pant leg.

Brought to the immigration bureau, Raynand is only able to make out a few of the sentences that mean, more or less, the end to a whole world of hopes and dreams.

– Go back! Go back to your fucking country!

Slivers of his most precious dreams fly away on the island winds, like the frailest bits of butterfly wings. Each one of those English phrases reminds him vaguely of that stupid eighth-grade English teacher who'd spent an entire year teaching the plural and the possessive.

– Get out of here! Son of a bitch!

Everything is slipping through his fingers . . . Destruction of an edifice he'd thought was made of solid concrete. Instead, it had been built of crumbly stone. God save the King! Poor Raynand! Leaf ripped off a dying tree. Mummy wrapped in bandages.

– Go back to your fucking country!

It's all over. Skinned alive. Total collapse. Complete disarray. The apocalypse brings down the last sections of wall in a whirlwind of blinding dust. Horrifying defoliation. A dry storm in the middle of the afternoon. Funereal journey of leaves migrating toward who-knows-what faraway places. A pile of books, swallowed down in class, that do nothing but irritate the brain. Soap bubbles that burst at the slightest angry wind. Useless brain. Gangrened hands. Destructive, insect-like fingers. That's the repulsive mixture you're left with after fifteen years of fastidious classical studies. Fifteen years of brainwashing. Fifteen years of bullshitology! The dramatic shipwreck of an entire educational system focused on the decorative and the folkloric. Absolute annihilation.

⁎　⁎　⁎

It was during the world war. The second one. Sometime in 1943 maybe. There were few radios in the working-class neighborhoods. Every night we rushed over to the house of a well-off neighbor who proudly made available his fancy new RCA

VICTOR *for the inhabitants of Bel Air. Even random passersby gathered around the front steps to follow passionately the latest international news. Our parents talked of bombs, of aerial offensives, of naval combats. We children lived paradoxically between total ignorance and fascination with the submarines, torpedo boats, armored tanks, and unmanned airplanes that peppered the conversation of the adults. In the end, the episodes of war, distorted by the popular imagination, seasoned with a dash of the marvelous, peopled our interior lives. Our heads were potpourris of nightmares and bloody dreams. Hitler was introduced to me by my cousin (who didn't really know much more than I did) as some sort of dragon, a magician. I took it to another level: for me, he was like the ghost of the invisible man, the white devil who disappeared and reappeared whenever he wanted and wherever he wanted. Waking at night to use the toilet, I was actually afraid that I'd find him in my room – with that lock of hair on his furious forehead and that nervous mustache. Despite our considerable distance from the front, the whir of any plane in the skies above Port-au-Prince made us shake in our boots. The thing was, Haiti – by way of her president, Élie Lescot – had just decided to ally herself with her generous neighbor Uncle Sam by declaring war against the Axis Powers Rome-Berlin-Tokyo, in the name of the sacred principle of Pan-American solidarity (which, over the course of history, had never managed to offer our hungry selves the slightest crumb from the great feast that might have happened to fall under the table of the Continental banquet). According to public rumor, Hitler had intimated that after Germany's victory he'd turn our little island, lost in the middle of the Atlantic, into a stable for his horses. Despite the lack of credibility of the idiot Lescot's unpopular regime, the Haitian people – with their glorious past – found their dignity profoundly insulted by this idea, and offered their blood to the cause of freedom and democracy, sending volunteers to the front and putting their territory at the disposal of the United States. And the denouement wasn't long in coming: spring 1945 solidified the defeat of fascism.*

In our neighborhood, Bel Air, there lived an Italian named Papito, a deserter from Mussolini's army. Taking advantage of the black market, he'd been able to make some money selling soap made out of guaiacum wood. On Sundays, he'd round up all the kids in the neighborhood and take them to the cinema. Later on, suspected of having tried to introduce us to the world of alcohol, cigarettes, and pederasty, he was more or less cast out of the community. At the end of the war, called to return to his country, he preferred to put a rope around his neck instead. After breaking down the front door of his house, the police found him hung on a beam, his eyes bulging, his face swollen with black blood. The neighborhood was completely shaken up, just like when Lescot first declared war on the Axis Powers at that time.

And I'm not sure why, but today these two facts are permanently linked in my memory: Lescot's unthinking bravado and the suicide by hanging of Papito the Italian.

■   ■   ≈

There are three hundred of them. Four hundred fifty. Eight hundred. Close to a thousand. In the corridors. In the hold. On the bridge. They're young. Old. Sad. Pensive. Taciturn. Chatty. They're there. Piled on the ship like so many pieces of damaged merchandise. A scrap heap of a boat chartered by the Bahamian governor to repatriate the mass of Haitian nationals living illegally in the various islands of the Bahamas. The wind blows strong. The waves break ferociously against the port side of the boat. Some of the refugees stacked on the bridge look out, at once nonchalant and livid, as the lights of Nassau fade little by little. It's seven thirty in the evening. The same situation. The same conditions. The same troubles. The same despair. An immense wandering heart. A misery without moorings.

They'd spent a month, two months, four months in the English prisons of the Bahamas before being stockpiled here, on this old ship headed for Haiti. No one knows exactly. A truly loathsome trip home. A backpedaling that no one had the slightest desire to make. Having come to these islands with a trunkload of hopes, they were headed back home today against their will. Hearts ripped apart in fear of what lay ahead. Hangdog souls. Suffice it to say, these travelers weren't at all happy to be seeing their homeland again. A few of them, slumped in a corner, showed absolutely no sign of life. Others took little steps to stretch their legs. There were those who spoke. Some under their breath. Some with voices raised. But all their secrets, all their accusations, all their mutterings, the wind, the uneven sea, the rolling of the ship, together formed a strange symphony of desolation. Drama of ultimate despair. Tragedy intensified by the bitterness of the women's sorrowful voices. A heartrending panting that reached up to the veiled backdrop of the sky.

– What can possibly await me there? The infernal welcome of atrocious suffering. Unbearable unemployment. Intolerable privations. And prostitution.

– I've lived thirty years of tribulations. That's why I seem so worn-out for someone who's only thirty-eight years old. I'm sure that, looking at me, you'd take me for fifty.

– In my whole life as a perfectly fit man, I don't believe I've worked more than thirteen months . . . as a carpenter in the Artibonite Valley. Ever since, walking day and night, looking everywhere for work, all my sap has been drained. Now I'm reduced to the dregs. No job. No profession. It would be one thing if I hadn't been looking . . . But still . . .

– I who thought myself brave enough to move mountains, who had the drive to take over the world! What have I become? A loser. A useless limb. A good-for-nothing wanderer. A vestigial organ.

– My infirm mother has no one but me to count on. Once upon a time she sewed, did laundry, ironed for people in the neighborhood. On Césars Street. But for a while now there's been no work. She's rotting away in her run-down cottage. In these hard times, everyone's doing his own sewing, laundry, ironing. In coming to Nassau I thought I'd be able to help her out and even get her old house fixed up. She'll never survive this. No question, she's simply going to die . . .

– Those days, nightlife didn't exist in Port-au-Prince. Everything was dead. From what I've heard, nothing has changed. The slump is still going. The cafés are moving in slow motion. Business is at a standstill. One good day . . . four bad days. The worst thing about it is that the Dominican prostitutes have taken over the best bars. Without the slightest effort they're replacing the Haitian prostitutes. Full of prejudice, the clients prefer those Spanish chicks for their thick, long tresses and their coffee-and-cream complexions. These foreigners are well paid. Sometimes up to thirty dollars a blow job. And to think, some of them are no better than mango leaves . . . Unequal combat where the black woman has her own brothers fighting against her. Haitian men are seriously messed up!

– There are times when you don't even have enough money to pay for food and rent. In the end, what more could I do – aside from be completely discouraged? Accept failure. Hunger. Death. What kills me now is that I have to go back without a cent. Shame on my grimy face.

– I left Môle Saint-Nicolas stowed away in the hold of a ship. Hidden among hundreds of sacks of rice and bunches of bananas. Just a year ago. Thanks to the help of a member of the ship's crew to whom I'd promised eighty dollars, I was able to get around the vigilance of the captain. Moreover, I'd have offered my very life to pay for the trip if necessary. Look at the ropey, bulging veins wrapping around my arms, my hardened hands, my fingers streaked with grooves and calluses. They've been useless, you know. I've wanted so badly to work. To be able to come home at night, muscles aching. To be able to say, pleased with myself, that I'd earned my daily bread by the sweat of my brow. To experience the satisfaction of having accomplished my task as a good father to my family. I had none of that . . . All that was left for me was begging. Theft. Pederasty. Corruption. Prostitution. My dignity sorely tested, I couldn't go on. I was at the end of my rope. Undone by idleness . . .

– All I have to do is start thinking, insofar as I can even manage that, and I start wishing for death. What's waiting for me . . . an ordeal without end. I'm already shaking. Unemployment. Hunger. Fear. Anguish. Nightmare from which there's no awakening. Paralysis of the tongue. Stiffening of the limbs. All that kills without mercy. And the rest of the footage for this film isn't very hard to imagine . . . Walking mummies. Individuals reduced to children. Zombies kept in line with whacks of a cudgel. Oh yes, zombies! We've all become zombies.

– What I've endured to make it here! I have no words to describe it . . .

– You've got to be kidding me! It tears me up inside to have to remember my own situation. And my memory has been bleeding during this whole relentless ordeal. We'll call it purgatory, if it's God's stick that's beating me – the horrors of hell, if it's the evil of men! The journey we went through, no way I'd ever have believed something like that possible . . . Nine of us had paid one hundred and fifty dollars up front to the owner of the bathtub that was meant to bring us to Nassau. A clandestine voyage for which we had to take every precaution, exercise maximum discretion. Sails flapping, we'd left the shores of Gonaïves one Tuesday at dawn. The day went by without incident. In the afternoon, we came upon a big, oblong boulder, shaped like a big loaf of black bread, a few scrawny mangrove plants grow-ing on its surface. The captain made clear that we were to get out there and wait for him for half an hour at most. To give him some time to contact his associate, he explained, a smuggler who usually assisted him in these sorts of schemes. In any case, he hastened to add persuasively, "My friend isn't far from here; he lives in the area, on one of these little islands; he's an experienced seaman; he knows his way around better than I do." And so we peacefully disembarked to wait for him. An hour went by, followed by several others. The bathtub was taking a long time to come back. Our eyes searched the darkness. Our voices trembled with fear. In spite of the cold and the humidity, we were resigned to spending the night on the boulder. Huddled together on top of one another in a compact mass. In a common anguish. With no cover. Suddenly, since we weren't sleeping, the sound of steps, like the rustling of dry leaves, caught our attention. We got up cautiously, guessing at what it could be. When we used our lighters, the horror of a bloodcurdling spectacle presented itself before us. A terrifying army of crabs had already invaded the entire surface of the boulder. Enormous, bulging, greenish crabs. Despite our screams, the noises we made to scare them, we were barely able to chase them away. Unbelievably, their numbers kept increasing. Incalculable hordes. They grasped at our pant legs. Scratched. Bit. I felt my legs swelling from their stings, bites, and scratches. We continued to battle them. But each time we managed to crush a few of them, more aggressive successors immediately launched an attack. A horrifying crunching of antennas, legs, blistering mouths. In the end, confusion took hold. Besieged. Disheartened. Panic-stricken. We jumped into the sea. Then, to top it all off, only five of us knew how to swim. We couldn't save the others, weak as we were, depressed, and fearful that the worst would happen to us too. After more than three exhausting hours of swimming and painful paddling through the waves, we were rescued – half-dead – by a patrolling lifeboat. We were given first aid. A week later, still suffering from shock, I found myself in a dark room with only a basement window providing air. To my great astonishment, I'd been shut away in a Nassau prison where I was to await my imminent repatriation to my home country . . .

– For me, hell is right here on earth. I've lived and suffered enough to know that. No one will ever make me think otherwise. I can't imagine a demon more intelligent, more ingenious than man in the perfecting of punishment and misery. And in the end, life is contained dramatically within the parentheses of an enigmatic choice. A miserable set of alternatives: furious wisdom or peaceful madness. Otherwise, of course, surely we'd be dead before we even started living.

Endlessly, the passengers speak whenever they aren't sleeping. Two nights and two whole days of navigation. Long hours woven with stories of misery and wandering, drawn-out sighs and a spattering of complaints. Voices thick with weariness and sadness against the calm silence of the sea. Hundreds of broken-down bodies on the old, wheezing ship. At dawn on the third day, the reflected rays of the sun illuminated the Caribbean. Large birds gleaming black and pink flew diagonally and heavily over the boat. In a few hours . . . Haiti. Enormous sharks followed in the vessel's frothy wake; their narrow, silvery fins cut through the blue waters of the Wind Canal. Everything seemed marvelous. The majesty of the ocean. The flapping flight of the birds that alight periodically on the yard. The leaping sharks. Nature's splendor. Unchanging. Eternal. Indifferent. As if it had never had anything to do with the suffering of men.

Standing up toward the rear of the deck with twenty or so other wretches, the unfortunate souls being sent back with him, Raynand seems to be lost in appreciation of this simple beauty, in a confusing amalgam of sensations and thoughts. To see my mother again. The streets of Port-au-Prince. The smells of humanity. The erotic heat. To return to this little place differently, in less pitiful circumstances . . . How happy I'd be! But to land back in my country as a good-for-nothing. Without money. Completely derailed. A wreck. Wearing this threadbare suit. Flapping in the wind. How will I be welcomed by my country . . . by my neighborhood . . . by my home?

Raynand's gaze floats above it all, faraway. Suddenly, he's torn from his daydreams by a sound that makes him start. A real racket. A veritable panic. In the front of the ship, anguished voices, begging:

– My friends, please, come back here! You're going to kill yourselves! Don't do this! Come back! . . .

Raynand barely has a chance to catch something about the escape and possible rescue of some drowning men before he realizes that there's a group suicide happening. Four passengers had dived brazenly into the tide full of voracious sharks. Immediately, on the captain's order, the old piece of scrap iron slows down. The sea, a roiling abyss, becomes an electric drum set, beating out a frenetic jazz rhythm. Violent intake of air. Locomotive with buzzing mucous membranes pitilessly kneading their prey. Hand brakes engaged. Swirling funnel in which the sharks, in a great red disorder, share pieces of arms, legs, and jagged flesh amongst themselves. Entrails and chests torn to bits. Not one scream is heard. All is submerged in a grating tumult of fins and froth. A horrible shredding of jaws, teeth, fangs, and tails. A porridge of effervescent colors and bloody turbulence. A sudden brewing of living, active ingredients in full eruption. An unbearable lyricism of purplish-blue stained with scarlet stripes. A massacre of slashed meat and exploded viscera.

Eyes peeled and fingers tensed on some rigging, Raynand holds his breath. Vertigo. He turns away and can just make out the distant shape of the island of Haiti, indolent and desperately denuded on the horizon. That very day, they'll all disembark on the wharf in Port-au-Prince. A long line of horrifying skeletons. Faces from beyond the grave. If it weren't for the frequency of the spectacle of repatriated boat people, one would take them for strange zombies escaped from some marine cemetery. From the inner port of the city they file out, two by two. Heads lowered. Attached to one another. As if made up like plague victims to act, against a realistic backdrop, in some scene from a dramatic opera. Quotidian theater of island violence. Tragedy of a people torn between secular suffering and the uncertainty of a dream without moorings.

■   ■   ■

Of course, our classical university schooling and our independent studies had opened the door to the world of beings and things outside ourselves, although we often arrived at dead ends. We'd learned a lot from that. To the point where we began to have doubts. To become conscious of our own ignorance. To renounce. To break. Slow meandering of a river whose mouth seems to vomit up the sea. Fermentation of the brain that yearns to create because the body is suffering and the heart is raging. In flying over the vast forests of History, we thought we glimpsed through a window – or at least guessed at – humankind's long itinerary. Thus fascinated by an impossible dream of a moon and a rainbow wound together in the deceptive, velvety darkness, feverishly drinking up the light planted behind a nameless day, caressing the breasts and the navel of a sexless woman, parodying the language of sewn-up mouths, seeking the raised lids of a face without eyes, dancing on the contorted legs of a broken puppet . . . why ever would we stop milking the midnight cow? We draw the new milk of anonymous days. We don't worry about the vastness of the dome that opens onto absurdity and nothingness. It has been put there on purpose to discourage us, this incessant back-and-forth between sickness and relapse. Let us borrow the nocturnal eye of the phosphorous lamp. The fiancée is there, sewing her bridal gown in the next room.

Nothing but sleepless nights and insomnia have dilated our pupils – from the last drop of rainfall to the first picked fruit! Heavy stride, magical caverns on the wings of ballistic engines. Miserable and perilous acceleration of History by an angel of light. A scout who heads up the caravan. Avant-garde that calls for revolution. A dramatic sneeze that decongests the blocked nostrils of time. For I take all revolutions to be the sneezes of History.

At school, I'd come across this word – History – wide as life itself, stormy as the sea. I was told so much about it that I got lost in a maze, having added so many crazy ingredients that I'd ended up with an indigestible and complex sort of bouillabaisse. Repulsive cat soup. Movement of a mobile whose path traces a closed curve. Journey of a celestial body in its orbit. Rotation around an axis. Abrupt and violent change of direction. While I knew full well that life was in fact open – irregularly – onto the branches of a rising spiral. To the point of vertigo. And that, ultimately, old bodies, worn-out hearts, and weary legs all end up part of a new universe, engorged with energy.

More and more teachers and books passed before my eyes, talking to me of revolutions! The miracle of Christianity. Demographic surges. Economic booms. New ventures in psychoanalysis. Surrealist quests. Marvels of modern science. Barriers broken down. Toussaint Louverture, Dessalines, Karl Marx, Victor Hugo, Rimbaud, Einstein, James Joyce, Apollinaire, Lenin (whom I loved from the very first encounter) were presented to me either as madmen, visionaries, or as embittered and bloodthirsty characters. And during the twentieth century all political movements sought, or so it seemed at least, the revolt of the masses. Whereas on the sidelines of all demagogic orchestration the truth still seems inaccessible and ambiguous.

However, in a little corner of my life, at the very core of my being, the image of something I experienced long ago has always remained fresh. A seemingly banal event. But one that I carry in me like a drop of light. This image is first to appear, emerging from its hiding place, as soon as I hear anyone speak of revolution. It's in January 1946. I'm nine years old. Standing under the little gallery of my house one Monday morning, I see an enormous agitated crowd of mainly young people coming up Docteur Aubry Street. Frightened, I clutch the porch rail. At the bend of Tiremasse Street, one of the protesters kneels suddenly, his face aflame, his arms flung open. And cries out over and over: Down with Lescot! Down with misery! Excited, my mother begins to scream the same words. I ask her what they mean. She tells me that this is the revolution.

Ever since, whenever I hear or pronounce this word, before putting together its fundamental elements, the very first image that comes to my mind is that of a frenzied crowd and a man, arms flung wide, screaming out his suffering against one of the Lescots of this world.

■ ■ ■

Raynand climbs up Monseigneur Guilloux Hill, the one leading up to the sanatorium. Tired, he has trouble dragging along his own disoriented body. He'd been left in a state of complete exhaustion after that unjust and horrific three-month incarceration. His head, swimming with calculations, weighs too heavy on his shoulders. Why keep looking, when life poses questions with no ready answers? Solutions are all out of reach. Since yesterday, I've been wearing myself out in vain looking for ten dollars to save my dying mother. Tuberculosis. Pulmonary hemorrhage. She'd been spitting up blood. Resign myself? How can I visit her at the sanatorium? Without bringing her anything? And the thing is, she's there because of me, poor old woman. She caught this illness while I was out of the country. Her spirit broke when she found out about my troubles in that foreign land.

Can one ever know the toll bitterness takes on the life spirit that surges through the networks of an interior architecture we're so proud of? The blood that courses through our veins. I still don't understand. It's clear I'll never understand anything. I've always been told: do this, don't do that. At home, old uncle Raoul doled out, left and right, advice I found so rational that it never occurred to me to question it even once. Old uncle Raoul died one rainy night, a skinny dog and a bottle of tafia on either side of him. Drowning in debt. Abandoned by his wife, Nellie. Buried as a pauper in a mass grave. He ended up alone in his own skin. Turns out he'd never understood much about anything either.

At school, the teacher theorized, and terrorized – screaming about the usefulness of the sciences until our eardrums just about burst. My boy, think about it: the straight line, parallel lines, symmetry, right angles, etc. It was just so marvelous, that shortest distance between two points. Today, all the lines are broken. The roads are blocked by brambles and barbed wire. The object is beyond the center. None of the images I see are real. All the mirrors are distorted. There's only a mocking, farcical caricature spouting unintelligible phrases against a gray sky. The mobile and incandescent arc of life presents such different angles to each vision, each minute. The sun doesn't have its image in the hearth; it burns and we sweat, at the mercy of steep roads that lead nowhere. Other than to the most hideous suffering. To failure. The horrifying solitude of a sanatorium devoid of any treatment for disease.

With tiny steps, Raynand climbs toward the entry stairs to the hospital, his head encircled by a huge iron ring. Fever burns his brain. He's always had a fever. His first contact with the world was a burning, devouring malarial fever. He'd had to miss a week at Saint-Martial Middle School, where he'd been enrolled in basic classes in the children's section. Upon his return, still recovering, and unable to express himself in French, a ridiculous smile and idiotic facial expression were his only response to dear Sister Félicienne, who'd wanted a note explaining his absence – a note that his illiterate mother wouldn't even have been able to write. That was so long ago. Yet that scene stayed fresh in his memory. There, too, he hadn't understood. And his little classmates had all laughed at him.

His mother relied on him at the time, she who didn't know – and couldn't know – what life had in store for her . . . She who didn't know that her son was crippled in both legs. Crippled by the struggle for existence, ever since his bitter childhood, he'd been good at hiding his crutches and his wooden legs. In fact, had he ever had anything worthwhile inside him? He'd only ever made the poor woman suffer, she who naïvely thought that putting her child in the Seminary, an institution of classical education run by Spiritain missionaries, would guarantee his success. It's the first step that counts, she thought. But the road is long, perilous, strewn with emaciated skeletons. A pile of skulls, femurs, clavicles, pelvises, digits, severed little bones. Hideously ugly cadavers. Travelers fallen in the middle of the mournful night before their pale eyes were able even to make out the lights of a distant dawn. So many had fallen. They had faith in the future. They had goodwill. They'd fallen in the midst of struggling. For my part, I didn't worry about it. I was more of a faithful servant of evil. Playing hooky . . . Coins slipped out from under the damask rug . . . The mahogany furniture I marred on purpose . . . The classic books I resold on Cathedral Place so I could buy cigarettes and alcohol. The money for school fees I spent on sweets . . . Truly, Mama had no idea that I didn't give a damn about catechism, sacred history, arithmetic, French grammar, all of it peppered with holy communions and fastidious prayer. And what has she gotten for it, my mother? What's left for her? A life sacrificed for absolutely nothing. A candle that goes out for lack of oxygen and a liter of blood. Nothing more . . . not even ten dollars for the necessary serum. Nothing for her but the inevitable annihilation.

Raynand is standing, more or less, at a north-facing window of the sanatorium. Near his mother, who's dying along with the last rays of the July sun. The internist is saying something about a rupture of the pulmonary vessels, a situation that medical science could address, if it weren't already too late . . . But Raynand's gaze floats over Port-au-Prince, spread out at his feet. Dives recklessly into the city in its petri dish. Rises back up toward the church bells. Lingers on the roofs of the big buildings. Follows Jean-Jacques Dessalines Boulevard. Flies up to the smoking chimney of the Hasco sugar factory. Takes in the Plain of the cul-de-sac. And throws itself into the sea where the light is slowly disappearing in a bloody sunset.

When he comes back to himself, to the vast white room of the sanatorium, the old woman Marguerite is already wearing the cold sandals
of eternal silence, fading away as discreetly as she'd come into being. For
once letting go of the self-effacing role she'd taken seriously to the very
end. Ridding herself of those dreams she'd always believed could be realized with God's grace . . . with her prayers . . . with her novenas . . . and
with the countless pilgrimages she'd made to all the churches in the city.

*   *   *

At seminary, I took communion every Sunday at the seven o'clock mass. Instead of
teaching me that this was a purely symbolic ceremony, the teachers saw fit to fill my
little kid's head with the idea of a God buried somewhere inside the host. And I was
supposed to swallow the divine cautiously, without it grazing my teeth. It contained
the body and blood of Christ. And it required some serious lingual acrobatics to
dislodge the circular wafer stuck to the roof of my mouth and bring it to my throat.

One morning, coming back from the Sacred Table, I surreptitiously took the
host out of my mouth and placed it on the armrest. Then, after having examined it
carefully, I put it back between my teeth and patiently chewed it – as I would have
done with a hard candy. I couldn't detect any hint of blood. Just to be sure, I licked
the palm of my hand with my moist tongue. Nothing appeared aside from a bit of
viscous spittle. I was puzzled. Disappointed, even. I spent the whole day thinking
about it. Questioning myself. Crying about it. Especially troubled because I couldn't
share with anyone the profane nature or the disastrous results of my experiment. I
suffered terribly and couldn't eat anything that Sunday. It was the first shock of my
life. A whole section of a marvelous edifice began to crumble amidst a thick cloud

of dust that, once it had died down, left a hideous void around me. Much later I realized that I just taken my first difficult step in the painful ordeal that leads to enlightenment, to true peace of the soul. Other facts arose that shook my faith in the teachings and practices of religion.

I left school one afternoon. Nearing the Cathedral, I was caught in a sudden downpour and obliged to take shelter inside the church. Hours passed and the rain kept coming down. At seven in the evening, a priest, followed by the sexton, came around. Ceremoniously, he reminded all those present that the doors to the church would be closing and that we would all have to evacuate God's house. I didn't wait for him to finish his sermon. I was the first to leave, braving the furious downpour. I arrived home soaked to the bone. My mother gave me some ginger tea. And she rubbed my chest. Despite these efforts, because of my weak bronchial tubes, I fell seriously ill and owe my life to an unending list of medical prescriptions.

In sixth grade, during the school holidays, I became passionately engaged in reading the Bible. I was floored to discover the existence, on every page, of a cruel and unjust God – a true despot who accepted Abel's offerings while disdaining those of his brother Cain. That hurt me. I suffered along with Cain. This poor peasant who knew how to till the earth. To sow seeds. To observe the germination and growth of plants. To make out the circulating of green sap in the branches. To pick the most beautiful fruits of his garden. To bring them to his lord and master. Only to be rejected with a slap in the face from He who desired a blood sacrifice. All of that marked me deeply. The inexorability of a god served by angels armed with double-edged swords. The shortsightedness of a vengeful and jealous creator driven to drown his work in a flood. And then his regret at having breathed life into man. All these pages revealed to me the monstrosity of a tyrannical and capricious God.

However, from as far back as I can remember, it was in philosophy class that I received the real sledgehammer argument (don't worry – I'm not going to bore you with the details of all my readings). Of course, I had gotten to know about History and about the great masters of scientific thought. I knew how Christianity had come into being and developed in the context of the slaveholding Roman Empire until it became the state religion. The Inquisition. The persecution of progressive thinkers. The discrediting of Epicurus, who wanted to free men from their fear of the gods. Giordano Bruno's auto-da-fé. Vanini's tongue ripped out. Galileo's sad story. Darwin's evolutionism. Marxist theory. Freud's discoveries. The theological and philosophical uncertainties of Teilhard de Chardin, who preferred talking about the noosphere and the Omega Point as expressions of divine transcendence, following which he should have logically posited, at the end of his scientific research, the spiritual dynamic of matter and the primacy of energy in all cosmic, physical, and biological phenomena. Of course, I knew all of that.

However, what struck me was a perfectly banal fact. It happened in 1955. High schools were going to the airport to welcome the American vice president Richard Nixon. I got into line with everyone else. Suddenly, at Grand Street, I was struck in the forehead by a rock that some kid had thrown at a dog pissing on the wheel of a car. With a black eye and the arch of my eyebrow slightly fractured, I had to leave the parade. Once home, I immediately placed a saltwater compress on the swollen wound. Plunged into bitter thoughts, I shivered at the idea that I easily could have lost an eye for no reason. I spent the whole day trying to find the causes that might have explained the fact that I'd been hit by this projectile. Why me personally and not someone else? I didn't find any convincing explanation. I also looked for what I might have done wrong, but couldn't point to anything. So it was that I began thinking about chance. Religion offered no decent explanation. Only scientific data came to my rescue and, just like that, I understood the laws of ballistics: understood, that is, the fact that I'd been walking in line, in step with the rhythm of my column; that the rock had been thrown clumsily, in accordance with its own speed; and, finally, that at one point I'd very logically become a specific target on the trajectory of the projectile. Sudden clarity. I'd seen the light. My heart beat more quickly. I forgot the pain in my head. Chance no longer existed for me. My thoughts extended outward to consider the sufferings of all those who seemed to be victims of some dreadful fate. Those who lived in slavery or misery. Peoples oppressed by wealthy nations. I began to understand it all. Underdevelopment. The appearance of political leaders, artists, scientists, geniuses. Beauty. Ugliness. Natural epidemics. Progress. Vices. Births. Wars. Victories. Defeats. Scientific discoveries. Works of art. From one thing to the next, the world unfolded before me, clear like water from a stone. Nothing stopped me anymore, since I'd found an explanation for all cosmic phenomena. I was now equipped to perform an autopsy on both happiness and sorrow. I left behind anthropomorphism and anthropocentrism any time I needed to analyze some particular occurrence or other. I considered man as one animal among many. And, courageously, I told myself that anything that can happen, good or bad, to any of the other species is just as likely for man. The only difference – a quite significant improvement, to be sure – is that we fully understand the situation! And even there, the keen awareness that we have these problems draws all its enlightenment from the blinding sun of science.

Since then, I look at religion as a trompe l'oeil for the naïve, a screen, a major obstacle to the objective study of human behaviors or any other phenomenon. And the idea of God, a cork to stop up who-knows-what hole. A hole that doesn't actually exist. Purely imaginary. That shouldn't frighten anyone.

For the universe is an infinite mass of energy. The void is only apparent as it is constituted by intermediary entities that rely on other unknown regions. New ones. Where man pursues his adventure in an interminable process at once continuous and discontinuous. Where light shines brighter and brighter. Takes us. Tears us away from the monotony of the quotidian. Throws a pure diamond into our hearts. And injects us with the virile audacity that makes this world move along.

■　■　■

A heavy day. Hot. Suffocating. Exhausting. Summer tunes its drums. Suspended by some invisible rigging, the sun, giant monster, casts its voracious tentacles on the rooftops, the streets, the bodies and blinding windows of the cars. Harshly. Ferociously, even. The sun doesn't grow old. Steadfast eye, it has become a roaming light. The day emerges from the trickle of tears gushing from the blazing eye of this wandering Cyclops. At times, a few stray clouds wipe at the dazzled corners of that eye whose every lash is the clash of a cymbal in the ears of the planet. The striking of a drumstick on the tanned hide of the islands.

Just after noon, the eye gnashes mercilessly. Arms itself with a circle of teeth that bury themselves deep into the bones of all things. Into the very heart of this so-fragile existence. Trees, animals, men cry for mercy. But the burning eye, bursting with vitriol, turns a deaf ear. It holds on to those fine rays that pierce, tear apart. Needlessly penetrating into our guts. Impassible judge, it watches the living as they slowly die. Who, then, could even speak of survival? That would be ridiculous. Who could possibly talk about relief while we find ourselves here at the very bottom of a seething boiler? Such talk could only leave us feeling more crushed, even more broken.

The streets stretch out, veins dried up, thinned out, bloodless. The sun has swallowed everything up. Leaving nothing but powdery earth under the steps of the aimless vagabonds. Throats that have given out from having yawned too much, begged too much, moaned too much. A streak of white dust on the asphalt traces the circle of death.

Blinding mirror that condenses the misfortune and doom of the idle pedestrians. Each face is pressured to pay up its share of sweat.

That afternoon, four young men are seated at the entry to a passage on Macajoux Street. Overwhelmed by the heat and by an overall sluggishness, they speak of everything and nothing.

Abruptly passing from one topic to the next, just to pass the time. Searching . . . in the void. A quest . . . into oblivion. A way of managing their boredom. From time to time, taking turns, they wet their lips, the tips of their tongues, their palates, with a little glass of sweetened rum. Filled three quarters of the way, the bottle, in which blond cherries and twigs of cinnamon are soaking, is placed underneath Raynand's chair. He's the most chatty, the least thirsty of the bunch. Paulin is there, too; he drinks moderately, but smokes quite a bit.

– It's a superior compound. Quite a nice little concoction. Been macerating for many days.

– Paulin, you've heard the latest international news. Seems like things are going from bad to worse in Southeast Asia. The escalation has crossed a new threshold.

– It's pretty serious. The Vietcong are about to launch a general offensive.

Passing the bottle around, each of them has a small glass. Raynand removes a packet of Splendids from the pocket of his shirt, takes out a cigarette, raps it quickly against the box of matches with light taps, then lights it and blows out rings of gray smoke.

– Roland is getting married on Saturday . . .

– Brave guy.

– How's that?

– He does nothing at all in life. Lifts neither light nor heavy loads. Neither straw nor stone. And he's getting married. Next Saturday. Not a day later.

– It brings tears to my eyes, just thinking about what he'll have to go through.

– You may be mistaken. Roland knows exactly what he's doing.

– Well, then, explain it to us.

– Roland's marriage – it's a transaction. A sort of investment. A misery insurance policy. But more than anything else, it's a dirty trick.

– Really, a dirty trick? You're not just saying that?

– Not at all. A suicide. Pure rubbish, really.

– Okay, now spill it. If you've got the goods, then let's hear what you have to say. Don't make us beg you for such small potatoes. We won't talk. And we've all got a pretty good poker face, so we won't give away anything you tell us.

– The girl is pregnant.

– So? Is that all?

– The kid isn't Roland's. The real father took off. He refused to marry her. So the girl's parents had the great idea to buy her a spouse. A sort of cover. Someone to wash her all clean.

– Now there's a story! This wouldn't happen to be something you made up?

– I'm telling you, Roland is a serious stain remover, the kind of detergent you use to get out the nastiest dirt.

– What are they offering him by way of compensation for plunging into such shit?

– The girl leaves for New York soon. Roland has wanted to go to the United States for a long time now. This marriage is the best deal he ever could have hoped for. It's the surest way for him to obtain a residence visa.

– So then that's the contract. The price of the soap. And then of course once married, he can be shown the door.

– Even if I were offered millions . . . there's no way I'd do it. For me – and I'm not even talking about a case like this one – marriage is a dangerous commitment. Single, I always know where to find my feet. I tell them to go left or right, and they obey me. Tied to someone, I'd never know for sure what my spouse was thinking. Or what she'd do at the moment when I'd count on her the most. When I'd count on her fidelity. Woman is an element of the unknown raised to the nth degree. We can live for three centuries and we'll never finish finding zeros to add on to that equation raised to the tenth power.

– So what do you have against women?

– Nothing, in principle. A lot, in practice. Enslaved for millennia. A commodity in bourgeois society. She isn't herself. In some cases an object of disdain. In other cases a degraded fetish. So my grievance is just as much with the society that has made women into a condensed form of all its problems. Married, one would live constantly with that stench in one's nose. And that causes nausea. And I don't like vomiting.

– And so, are you against marriage?

– I'm against living together, legal unions, and common-law arrangements.

– So what solution do you propose?

– Women must fight. Participate. Her autonomy mustn't be a gift. But a conquest. Only her active presence can change her situation. Neither laws nor decrees are going to earn her real emancipation. Only her participation in the liberation of oppressed classes, of trampled-down races, can truly lead to her rehabilitation. She's got to give up all the self-pity and facile romanticism. She's got to stop begging. Put her shoulder to the wheel. And take what's owed to her. Not be satisfied with her status as spoil of war shared between men. A trophy for the victors. At the very least, give revolt a try. Not with moaning and supplications. She must assert herself to the world based on her own merit. Not by ruse or low blows. Strike head-on. Not from behind.

– Okay. You say that women must participate. For that, she'll have to stand beside men.

– Yes, beside men. Everywhere. In the most dangerous places. In the resistance movements. In the trenches. Coming close to death. Living it, not suffering it. Standing, by our side. Before lying horizontal on some bed. And all that depends entirely on her. We do not refuse her participation in those ways. On the contrary, we welcome it.

– All that outside of marriage?

– Outside all affective liaisons. Outside any household. Otherwise, it becomes a tomb in the end. We men must learn also to see women in a different light, less unhealthy, less perverse.

– In the end, you condemn love . . .

– No. I'm far-sighted. I issue a warning. Besides, in our current context, love – that marvelous sentiment, that vertigo that brings two beings together – only exists as long as those beings don't live under the same roof. As long as they haven't become materially intertwined. It's neither the man nor the woman's fault. It's the whole society's responsibility. On slippery ground like ours, the furniture to change, the wardrobe to update, the car and its mechanical problems, sicknesses, medications, jewelry, perfumes, and even the spice rack – all that leads to the strangulation and, ultimately, to the death of even the most powerful love.

– In that case, Paulin, you won't have children?

– The way things are right now, I wouldn't want to have any. I plan to remain available, for the time being. Children are a bunch of fruit hanging on beautiful flowering branches, yes, but too often they hold back the fervor of the tree. Whereas I intend to do with my life as I see fit. Too often, children amount to a long tail that hinders all movement. That keeps you from stepping over the fire. That makes you too cautious. The spouse, the good family man is a sort of mole who retreats into his den, where he thinks he can find safety for himself and his loved ones . . . False security! The hearth would be a constraint for me. A sort of underground tunnel. Whereas wide-open spaces attract me irresistibly. Have you never noticed with what ridiculous eagerness married men abandon the company of their friends for fear of encroaching on the hour or so reserved for the little wife?

– Really, Paulin, you wouldn't like to be married someday?

– I've often thought about it. And it repulses me, the pitiful little puppy dog trapped in the bond of marriage.

– Raynand, tell us what you think of your friend Paulin's ideas. Why don't you say a thing or two on the subject . . .

Raynand carefully fills his glass to the brim, takes his time emptying it, then responds calmly.

– To be afraid of marriage is a form of cowardice. I'm not denying the difficulty of domestic life, with a wife and kids, not one bit. On the contrary . . . But I see, despite that, important reasons to fight for such things. The life of a family man is made up of everyday heroism. Who doesn't recognize the valor it takes for a man to feed his children, to clothe them, to watch over his companion, to concern himself with her happiness, to give meaning to her life?

– Exactly, responds Paulin confidently. That's what I fear the most. Under no circumstances would I want to exhaust my own strength in fruitless battles. Not to mention all the petty conjugal disputes. A bit of warfare between lovers, as Sartre might say. There are so many problems to solve that I wouldn't want to dissipate my reserves of energy – out of affective lack or unforgivable weakness – on a woman who wouldn't understand my sacrifices. I loathe wastefulness. Moreover, as I've made clear here, in the best of circumstances, marriage consecrates the triumph of self-ishness in the illusory happiness of a closed circle. Removed from others and their suffering.

– You're a cynic, Paulin. The selfish one is you, who refuses to share your life, retorts Raynand angrily. Yes, you're the selfish one. You're afraid. Because you're not sure of yourself.

– Well, who isn't afraid? Who is sure of himself? Please, introduce me to this heroic being, this rare species of animal.

– I still love Solange. I'd marry her in a second, if she wanted that.

– Go after her, then. Marry her. Share your life with her. That's all up to you, if you're so sure of yourself.

– As far as this is concerned, Paulin, we'll never agree. We don't have the same history. Our experiences are different.

– Do you really want to brag about that, dear man? responds Paulin ironically.

Nonchalantly, Raynand rises from his seat. He downs another shot. Clasps his friends' hands. Gives Paulin's shoulder a friendly slap.

– All right, Paulin. I'm headed out. I'll come by your place tomorrow afternoon. I'll be there for sure.

– Okay, I'll be waiting for you. I hardly ever go out. I write. I'm preparing a great work.

Raynand goes out into the sun as it tips its fiery boiler into the bay. Above the din of the Croix-des-Bossales market, sailboats rest at anchor in the harbor. Butterflies perched on an immense gray platform. Ah, the silvery mirror that is the blue sea of the islands on a summer afternoon.

■ ■ ■

– *How many times did you tell me you'd come back! Every day I watch the trees gather up their shadowy skirts, propped up on their crooked legs. Every night I've counted the hours till the cock's crow, till the stridulations of the crickets. But you never came back, Jastrame.*

She lowered the flame of the lamp and lit a candle that she'd affixed using a bit of wax melted on the little oak table. She undid the white handkerchief that held back her long hair, the color of cane syrup. Stretched out on a mat woven out of dried leaves from the trunk of a banana tree, I pretended to sleep. She couldn't know that I'd heard her, that I'd been watching her. Enlarged, deformed against the earthen wall, her shadow offered a pitifully disheveled image of unrequited love. She uncorked a flat bottle, spilled three healthy measures of spirits at the foot of her bed.

– You never came back, Jastrame. Can it be that you've abandoned me for the rest

of my days? Lord, why have you burdened me with this test too great for my strength and my morale? I suffered so much during my youth that I thought misery would have been forever banished from my existence. Lord Jesus! Mother Mary, my mistress! Why leave yet another vulnerable place in my brutalized heart?

Head bowed, she begins to weep. Until she's been worn out. Exhausted. To my eyes she'd become the very picture of suffering – weeping, naked, slumped on the armrest of the night. I stopped watching her. And I began to cry under my sheet. I cried all night long.

Grandmother, seventy years old at the time, never again saw Jastrame, her lover, her companion in old age. Alone in an impoverished province, cut off from her people, only seeing her grandson during the summer months, she died of despair. When we learned of her death, by telegram, the entire household burst into tears. During the two days spent in funeral preparations, I stayed clear of all the others, with their yapping like rabid dogs . . . Their cries bothered me. I didn't shed a single tear. They called me cynical, an ungrateful little beast incapable of affection. I didn't defend myself at all. I alone knew how much Grandmother had suffered in her solitude, because I had cried alongside her, without her knowing it, at the very moment where she needed – more than ever – to hear a human voice. Abandoned in her provincial hole, she'd spent her final days awaiting a touch, a word, a smile, a cry. Hoping for someone, a Jastrame, anyone. She died with only love's painful shadow to keep her company, tragic portrait of solitude projected on an earthen wall. That, I alone knew.

The day of her funeral, the truck in which we were riding swerved suddenly and flipped over near "Smelly Springs." Although no one was hurt, the accident itself upset me greatly. And I was even more horrified by the fact that my Grandmother would end up buried in a cracked coffin. Only eight years old, I'd already been made aware of life's cruel workings. With all its problems. Its surprises. Its complications. I knew that something didn't work correctly. I couldn't accept the fact that misery had been long nipping at the heels of a poor peasant woman, and had ruthlessly pursued her to her very grave.

Now that I have so much better understood Grandmother, I wonder if I'm not the only one in the family to keep an inheritance of torments and worries buried deep inside. In my body, sealed-in pain. In my heart infused with the tears of a night when love pitifully projected its lonely and fateful shadow on an earthen wall. Like Grandmother, I'm waiting for someone. Anyone. A touch. A human voice. A face. A Jastrame. I'm waiting to no longer be alone.

■   ■   ■

Three in the afternoon. Raynand is at Paulin's house, in his bedroom. He's clearly surprised by the atmosphere of silence and order that suffuses the little gray room. He's impressed. So astonished that he can hardly speak. He doesn't know where to begin. Not in a million years would he have imagined such discipline from someone as noisy and explosive as Paulin. He glances quickly at the shelves of the bookcase before sitting down. A bunch of marked-up manuscript pages have been arranged on a metal table.

– Are you the one who wrote all of that, Paulin?

– I've been working on a novel for the past few months. It's been tormenting me mercilessly, beating me like a draft horse. I've been carrying a heavy load ever since I took on this project.

– You say you've been working on it for months now?

– This could even take years, my dear Raynand.

– I've heard that the novel is a difficult genre.

– Yes, in a sense, rather difficult. Especially when it comes to breaking with tradition. To renewing something. To creating. Literature is beginning to grow old. And having arrived at this state of decrepitude, it risks being dethroned by cinema, which, conversely, shows brand-new vigor. Making use of the scientific technologies of the twentieth century, and using the resources of other branches of the arts as helpful tools, cinema has achieved almost a miracle: it has raised itself to the level of a total art form. The threat it poses to literature is enormous. Certain. Yet it isn't a question of doing battle, or of eradicating it. That would be a waste of time. Literature is dying. It will die, without question. Not even the most seasoned doctors can save it. Its tissues, its arteries are sclerotic. And its heart, having turned into rusty metal, feebly pumps out rotten blood.

– If that's the case, what's there to do? I'd say you should stop writing. You might as well break that useless pen in two and then tear up these sheets of paper before throwing them in the fire.

– What's left is waiting for the end; the death throes can go on for some time. In the interval, literature will accept its place as underling. And we can still slow down its ultimate end by infusing this old, ailing organism with a bit of new blood. With something enriched that has been extracted from the drama of its own dying, which is also that of men – for whom the earth is no longer enough. The planet has become a straitjacket for man's respiration. He needs wings to rise up. To conquer infinite illuminated spaces. But literature, that decrepit old man, loses its breath in the course of such vertiginous ascension. And free falls terrify it. In the meantime, cinema, marvelously new, served up by the television and by communication satellites, quickly travels along the new itinerary of cosmic waves. That's why, my friend, to produce a literary work that pays close attention to the aesthetic becomes so difficult. Originality, authenticity – these are the stumbling block and the challenge. We must create, more now than before. As we wait for the certain turn toward death. The fascinating era of interstellar acrobatics.

Raynand is spellbound by Paulin's words. After a few moments of contemplation, he lights a cigarette.

– Tell me, Paulin, how far along are you with your novel?

– The first chapters are already written. I'm at a crucial point, and I'm finding it very difficult to move forward. It happens at times that I end up spending hours doing battle with a single blank page. A cruel sheet of paper that refuses to fill up. That stubbornly refuses to bear the scratch marks of my pen or the strikes of my typewriter. A resistance that undermines my spirit. Often reduces me to tears. Because in such moments, neither semantics nor the dictionary, nor grammar, nor memories of past reading are of any help. And so, I give it up. I get into my bed and tell myself that literature is a curse. The surest path to my self-destruction. To suicide. But then the next day, I wake up full of enthusiasm. And I go back to writing, like a rebel full of rage. A masochist full of vices. An incorrigible megalomaniac. A *zo-bouke-chen* – irredeemably shameless!

– So what is it that holds you back?

– It isn't that I don't know what to say. It's the way of saying it that torments me. The obsession with language in the crucible of solitude. Writing is the stumbling block. There are moments when I feel the weight of several tons pressing down on my shoulders. And then I lose my breath. And the clutch slips. I think that's where the essential difference lies between painting and music, on the one hand, and literature, on the other. The basic instruments used by the painter and the musician to communicate their ideas – that is, colors and notes – are external and allow for easier manipulation. Whereas the writer has no direct grasp of words, which are completely internal. The painter has before him his palette and the whole range of colors. The musician, his instrument, and the panoply of scales and registers. As for the writer, he must constantly risk an incursion into the interior volcano, in order to extract, burned by lava, even the simplest word.

– I think I understand a little. So, Paulin, what's the subject of your novel? What's the title?

– I haven't started worrying about the title yet. That will come, I'm sure. For the time being, I'm sorting out the structure of the chapters.

– But what are you going to talk about? You must have a story to develop.

– Not one I have the least idea about. Look, I don't want to write a narrative novel. Or a story that goes from one end of a straight line to the other.

– If I understand what you're planning, you'd like to try out the experiment André Gide conducted in *The Counterfeiters*?

– Not exactly . . . More like expand it. Gide composed his novel *en abyme*.

That, of course, already marked some measure of progress in the construction of the novel as a genre.

– And what do you plan to do?

– The novel is a vision of life. And as far as I know, life isn't a segment. It isn't a vector. Nor is it a simple curve. It's a spiral in motion. It opens and closes in irregular helices. It becomes a question of surprising at the right moment a few rings of the spiral. So I'm constructing my novel in a spiral, with diverse situations traversed by the problematic of the human, and held in awkward positions. And the elastic turns of the spiral, embracing beings and things in its elliptical and circular fragments, defining the movements of life. This is what I'm using the neologism Spiralism to describe.

– Okay. Still, you're not going to make me believe you're writing this novel without even the slightest idea of where it's going.

– I don't have even the slightest idea. No fixed notion should hold back the breath of a work that reproduces the accelerations and the imbalanced spasms of life. I take the pulse of the spiral and inscribe it in graphs and charts, from the very life of writing. It's a pluridimensionality at the level of words – words functioning as particles of sonoric energy in motion.

– Well, if that's the case, your novel seems to be based on pretty expansive foundations. Which puts an extremely vast area of exploration at your disposal, I suppose. An immense field you can draw from at will.

– Not exactly. To say that I'm developing the theme of bankruptcy would be inexact. Rather, I suggest an ambience of failure. Writing a thermometer-novel capable of indicating the temperature of fictional landscapes. Making it so that the reader feels the climactic and spatio-temporal variations.

– I fear, Paulin, that you're going about it all wrong. That you're following the wrong path. That the public won't understand.

– The public will understand. In fact, that's who I'm writing the last chapter for. Does one have to be a genius to know if the weather is good or bad, if it's night or day, if it's cold or hot outside? Everyone knows, with no fear of getting it wrong, when it's raining and when it's sunny. That's why, theoretically, I won't explain anything to my reader. He'll make out the landscape by the ambient temperature that touches his senses directly. He'll play along from the start. What's more, I'd like the dialogue between characters in the Spiralist novel to recall that of the theater, and for it to be situated right at the limits of poetry.

Raynand realizes this is one of the rare moments in his life where he's hearing someone speaking with conviction. Paulin's voice resonates more seriously than usual. It was as if the room were being lit up by his presence. By his words. As if all the light were surging up from the very depths of his wild eyes.

– What obsesses me the most is the idea of escaping from the bunker that imprisons every one of us. Of conveying who I am by deciphering the hieroglyphics that hamper my vision. The enigmas that exasperate me. By managing to trigger something in the reader's thoughts. The manipulation through writing that would create a communicative field and force people to move outside of stereotypes and normalcy.

– For that, Paulin, you'll need an accessible language.

– Not necessarily accessible from the start. I present my language in the dizzying circles of a fabulous merry-go-round. Magic carousel that sometimes spins against the wind. It's a moving polyhedral mass. Changeable. I loathe the Procrustean bed.

– Okay, so you already must have conducted some linguistic experiments, since you seem, as far as I can tell, to accord great importance to writing. To the formal.

– Obviously. The writing process is the work. You might say it's equal in density and scientific weight to the literary work. That's why I'm against writing that's presumptuously neutral and objective, and against the unoriginal. As to the formal, it's equally inseparable from the whole of the work. It neither precedes nor comes after it. It is during. Throughout. From one end to the other. It is neither an envelope nor a garment. It's a certain expansion of creation within a given space and at a given time. As such, it would be fundamentally artificial to pose the old question of form and content. The traditional approach that separates matter from spirit. That would amount to imagining a prefabricated model. Exhibited in a store window. However beautiful, it's being worn by a wooden, rubber, or plastic mannequin. Without life.

– In this, you've opposed yourself to anything that seems too normal, too traditional . . . huh! I suppose you could say, anything too classic.

– A bit of that, yes. For example, for the Spiralist novel, style would play the role of barometric register. Endowed with infinite variability. Capable of indicating the most unexpected atmospheric variations. From that point on, the word attains its greatest autonomy. Inflated with meanings. Swollen with allusions. Amplified by the cross-references it implies. The word, freed of the tutelage of the sentence, gains in depth and breadth. And what's more, it gives the impression of speed. A facility of acceleration. The word must fully enjoy its associative virtue. Inserted with precision into a sentence, the word becomes a sort of slave and thus loses its nerve, its lifeblood. Often, in a work nourished by the imaginary, the transparent amounts to a reductive element, an impoverishing factor. A narrow corset that suffocates fiction. The word, lacking the necessary space, atrophies. In desiring to tame the word, even the most well-constructed sentence turns it into a dead sign, because it's reduced to a single meaning. Whatever the word, it's always emptier in the middle of a sentence than it seems to be in reality. But when left to roam on its own, written or spoken, the simplest word acquires the richness of the swinging single with a world of partners to choose from. Whereas, in the context of a sentence, it once again becomes the pallid spouse stuck in the heart of a family with the mother of his children hanging on. Thus it often happens that I enclose a single word between two periods, so as to make it new, more powerful. Faster. More evocative. Richer. It's a new kind of sentence. Created with the help of a lexeme that plays the strange role of the un-stable kernel, perpetually popping. I call this an undulatory sentence. Like a stone thrown onto the surface of a lake, it sets off interior waves that make innumerable connections with the lived experience of the reader or the listener. It is the very basis of the Spiralist language.

    – Paulin, I predict some pretty serious outcry against these concepts of yours – you'll be accused of hermeticism. Or of madness. Even more so because they give off a strong odor of sulfur.

– Not a big deal. I won't die from whatever reception I get. Time is on my side. That's good enough for me. I own my dissidence.

– So you'll stick to your guns, despite everything.

– Yes. Come hell or high water. I'm betting everything on the Spiralist aesthetic. It could help resolve most of the problems in art. Particularly that of language.

– Okay, Paulin, so you're talking about the crisis of language that's facing contemporary literature.

– Of course, Raynand. It's a part of the more general crisis.

– Strictly speaking, how does this crisis appear in the literary realm?

– Through a certain inadequacy . . . a phase shift.

– Paulin, I just don't know what you mean by that.

– I'll explain. Certain words. Certain expressions. As a result of being brooded over. On everyone's lips. On everybody's tongues. Soaked in drool. They end up being veritably eroded, left with nothing more to say. Having become insipid flakes of sawdust that pass ridiculously from one mouth to the next. Empty speak. The preferred style of whores and demagogues. Inflationist and idiotically anecdotal writing. These days, more than ever before, we're raising the question of language. Tragic. Painful. Faced with intellectual consciousness. How can the distance between speech and gesture – between word and act – be eliminated, or at the very least reduced? How can the dichotomy that so often affects speech and action – positing one against the other – be resolved? In my humble opinion, Spiralist language –

endowed with mobility, capable by its functionality of suggesting an ambience, of sensing the temperature – could, by dynamiting intuition, offer a chance to avoid the trap of figurative sterility. It's time to liberate literature from the dictatorship of dictionaries and grammar books.

– You're not worried that the spiral could degenerate into a banal circle that would end up distancing you from reality?

– Raynand, allow me to speak to you frankly. The world we live in is full of problems. My work must bear witness to this era. If blood is the price to pay, I'll be careful, yes. But I'll never give in. I'm disgusted by lame heroes. That being said, art mustn't be confused with exhibitionism. It's got to be entirely distinct from the croaking of frogs and the yapping of jackals.

– Paulin, would you permit me to ask a slightly indiscreet question?

– No objection. Go ahead.

– How many pages will this novel end up being?

– I don't know exactly yet. But what I'm sure about is that it won't be more than three hundred pages long. And I'm going to stick to that.

– Why is that?

– Because in our time, I find that those novels that go on and on are irritating and are only ever read superficially, and by a limited public. Literature is already dying. Supplanted by the sonorous and visual universe of cinema, which has stolen the strongest part of its voice. Moreover, its audience shouldn't be hobbled; that would only accelerate its horrifying and tragic death throes. Filmic images and sound waves achieve the miracle of not boring the public by transmitting the message within a limited time and in a relaxed atmosphere. Of gregarious communion. And tomorrow, when man will have put in place numerous relay stations on the routes of rocket ships, like it or not, nothing will escape the magic of telecommunication. Our age doesn't lend itself to reading literary works, boring in their too often useless length. We no longer live in the century of the wig-wearing, stay-at-home salonists who wall themselves up at a remove from the swirl of humanity. Between the fatigue of the night before and that of the day after, the worker, the technician, artisans, the laboring classes only have limited time – if they have any at all – to read printed characters. And even the unemployed are preoccupied with the more urgent problem of dinner. And so, it's a question of stating things quickly. Without uselessly dragging out the dialogue. Without encroaching on the schedule. In this world of speed, where events unfold at a dizzying pace, faster is better. Otherwise, the book's days are numbered and its adventure hurtles toward the point of collapse and dissolution. In this world so fabulously turned upside down by first-rate technology, where any sense of balance has become fleeting, the writer risks becoming outmoded, lacking the ability to adapt. All this explains why Spiralism is the most appropriate vision for this cosmic whirlpool.

– When will you be able to finish your novel?

– I'd like to be able to finish within the next six months. Unfortunately, I only write at night . . . when the interior demon of creativity roars. Aside from this handicap, I don't write in a single stroke. I can't produce cold. Whirlwinds. Vertigos. Storms. My life beats to the rhythm of turbulences. I am a Spiralist. And voluntarily I flee tranquillity, sterile and frigid. It brings with it the sign of death, the insignia of a mediocre life. I flee the monotony of repose and anything that resembles the straight and narrow. It's not that I'm looking to be scandalous. But because life itself emerges from the cry of blood. Wayward child of pain. Of violence. And that, too, is Spiralism. And the entire universe has embarked on the infinite movement of the spiral.

– Paulin, mind if I make a slightly harsh comment?

– I'm listening.

– Your theories are riddled with contradictions.

– Raynand, my friend, we live in a world in the middle of a metamorphosis. A universe of uncertainties. Life itself appears to be a cinema of illusions. Truth, always fleeting, often takes refuge in the opposite of what we call reality. Me, I've chosen to practice the paradox and the aesthetic of the aleatory.

Paulin is quiet for a moment. Gets up. Takes his pipe from a formica shelf. Fills it with tobacco. And carefully sparks the purple flame of a lovely little yellow lighter. Agitated, he inhales two successive puffs. The suave aroma of the tobacco invades the room in the silent escalation of the gray smoke as it rises to the cardboard roof. Raynand looks at his watch. Stands up. Stretches his arms up above his head. Moves toward the door.

– Okay, then. Paulin, I'm leaving. I'm going to the Rex to see this week's film. I need a break. In any case, I thank you for this afternoon. I'll be back. I'm intrigued by everything you've said.

– I'm at your disposal, Raynand. I'll be waiting. Let's stay in touch. I'm always here in the afternoon.

Passing by the bookcase, Raynand stops for a moment. Looks at a large photo of a smiling woman, positioned on the upper shelf. At the bottom and next to the woman's heart, Raynand calmly reads the dedication written in pen: "To my beloved Paulin, with my unchanging love. Sincerely, Marina."

– Hey, Paulin. Seems like you really love this one. If this picture is any indication, she's quite beautiful."

– Yes . . . very beautiful.

– All right, I'm going to head out now. I'll be back to see you some afternoon. Next week.

Raynand rubs his head with the flat of his hand. Takes off. And then disappears around the corner of a little street that somehow recalls the irregular arc of a half-bent elbow.

Paulin returns to his room. Pensive. He stands up next to the bookcase. Chin leaning against the edge of the shelf where the smiling photo of Marina is posed. He looks at it for a while. Backs up a bit. Looks at it again. More intently. A large medal pulls on the necklace hanging from Marina's neck. Her cheeks are rosy, flush with freshness and good health. A pair of triangular earrings. Two beauty marks. A little dot of brown flesh on the right nostril. Her delicate lips, made to measure, slightly parted to reveal a brilliant row of white teeth. Her hair like a flower crowning her wide forehead. Island Marina with her slanted eyes! Paulin looks at her. Even more deeply. Desperately. Passionately. His eyelids raise. His eyes widen with sudden illumination. The frame of the photo grows disproportionately larger. The cardboard rectangle bends into a curve. Pushes against the glass. And Marina comes alive, stepping gently out of the photo. Standing in the middle of Paulin's room. Smiling. Her back against the wall.

– Marina, do you love me?

– I cannot love. Because of men, my mother suffered her entire life. She is a slave to my father. And I don't want to be a slave to anyone. I lived up close with the cynicism and nastiness of men. They all behave like despots when it comes to women. Me, I . . . don't want to love anymore. I want no part of such a prison.

– You live curled up like a snail. In the end, you're the one who's built a prison for yourself. To protect yourself from a world you find too aggressive. You cultivate your mother's disappointments in yourself. You've made a shell for yourself and closed yourself up within it. Avoiding all contact with the world, which, in your eyes, has your father's face.

– Is it my fault if I feel like I'm made of ice?

– The ice that's hardened your heart is nothing more than a fear of confronting life. In fact, you're not really living. You're fast asleep. Having chosen, like a coward, to live life in slow motion, like a hibernating animal. Do you think life will have meaning after your death? It won't and it won't have been worth anything for your fellow creatures, your brothers and sisters who suffer. Because you won't have been anything more than an obscure absence in the great human adventure.

– But what would you have me do? You think it's easy to be present, to not live on the margins?

– You, you're not living at all. You don't dare. You choose to flee to save your honor. You always pull back whenever you think you're about to do something foolish. You're afraid of being born. Of knowing yourself. Of acknowledging yourself. Yet life is right there, and it goes by without waiting for you. The alternative is tragic. Live or die. And if you choose to live, you can't not make mistakes. Only death is infallible.

– I have no desire to live chained to evil and suffering until dying, in the end, like a dog.

– If it happens that I die like a dog, I'll have no regrets . . . I will have lived to the fullest my dog's life.

– With some other dog faithfully attached to your feet to keep you company.

– I'm not chaining you to me, Marina. I'm merely extending an invitation.

– But, Paulin, might not that invitation be selfishness in disguise? Might you be trying to satisfy your own pride?

– You call me selfish. You're wrong. I'm suffering. I'm tortured. Shattered. Crazy with the need to give my love. My weakness. My strength. My worth. I exist. I live. I'm present. I measure my weight in pain and joy. The scale's needle veers off course. It's no longer calm. Even in my deepest nights, my eyes shine far more than the wan paleness of death.

– You want to give me your life? All of it . . . Every last drop . . . Do you really believe we can be the exception to failure? That we can escape total collapse?

– Marina, believe me. I love you. I won't leave this world with anything at all. Much less with love, which cannot be hoarded.

– And if I accept? What would you ask me to do?

– To hold my hand as we travel new roads together. Risking our lives in stormy places. We need one another.

– Paulin, you think we'll overcome all obstacles, that we'll make it to the end? Is that a sure thing? Reassure me, I'm begging you.

– Marina, don't let conformity plant its evil flag in you. Death is conservative. Join me in taking the first steps to tear down the old ways, the patina of a universe paralyzed by normalcy.

– I love you too, Paulin. I've always forced myself to hide that from you. Today, I can't do it any longer. I love you. It's just that you're so violent . . .

– Violence isn't the thing to fear. Love smolders most powerfully in a storm. It's the moment when the tempest calms that should be feared. That would mean the death of our love.

– I know that only too well. I've long been aware that your life is not about still waters. Even your love is a raging sea on which only those with strong stomachs dare venture.

– Do you think you've got a strong stomach?

– I'll have to give it a try.

– You've got it right. Because I'm not promising you a path blanketed with flowers. My current existence may be couched in relative stability. But who knows whether tomorrow will be filled with privations . . . With persecutions? With torments? A man's path is not often strewn with roses and laurels. I have no idea yet what my life has in store for me. Each day calls for its portion of blood and sweat.

– I'm well aware. Paulin, this heart that I've never resigned myself to offering to anyone else – I'm handing it over to you without any precautions. Even if I end up suffering for it. I'll regret nothing. I am yours entirely. You've already tamed me.

– No. That must never happen. I would despise you. Never forget this word of advice: always keep your exchanges equal with your man. Never crawl on your belly. Never let yourself be tamed, not even by me.

– Not even by you, Paulin?

– By no one. Men have a tendency to consider women their private property . . . Don't you swallow any of the nonsense that comes out of their mouths. Whatever the cost, avoid becoming one of those women who contents herself with having her belly, her uterus, and her abdomen filled up. That kind of woman is only worth anything when she's horizontal.

– I thank you, my darling.

– Marina, do you know that I've begun writing my next novel? I've already written two chapters. I haven't found a title for it yet.

– When might I read a few passages?

– As soon as you'd like. You know that I owe my work to you. I've elected you queen of my creation. And your dynasty is eternal. I owe you all the works that are already scratching at my brain and nipping at my entrails. Marina, be the midwife to my works. Participate in the fascinating creative adventure that obsesses me. Straddles me. And violates me. I carry and sustain a perpetual pregnancy. I expect you to assist me in the miracle of birth.

The room darkens. Paulin is covered in sweat. His fingers, his lips tremble. His body shivers. A steamy vapor trickles out of his mouth, his nostrils, his eyes. Suddenly, he sees only black.

– Marina, make it bright in here. I'm begging you. Switch on the lamp. Give me your hand so I can make it through the tough times. Help me. I need you so badly.

– Alas, Paulin. My father knows we love each other. He's furious. My parents disapprove. They're sending me off to Europe. In twenty-two days. Like a package.

– It isn't possible!

– They've already taken the first steps.

– Marina, tell them that our love is a spring on the verge of becoming a torrent. That our love burns the eyelids and rips apart the eardrums of those who doubt it.

– There's nothing we can do to stop them. They are absolutely set on me leaving.

– Marina, I was born through your gaze. You delivered me in a bright flash of fire. Whether I live or die is up to you.

– Paulin, we must take this separation as a test. We'll come out of it victorious. Even more attached to one another. I'm confident. In exiling me far away from you, they will not get the better of us.

– My rebellious suffering, I'll cradle it in my lap. But for how long?

– It's possible that I'm to spend four years far from you.

– Four years! Here it is that, despite myself, I'm compelled to measure time's passage. Clocks, calendars – I hate them with a passion. The mutilation of days with their strange names that fracture our existence. That fracture life. Not to mention, is human existence really measurable in figures?

– Don't forget that time passes quickly. I'll come back. A trip won't be able to kill our love.

– Since you must leave, I'll ask one thing of you: believe in the possibilities of your country. Come back to it. The black man doesn't easily get comfortable in the land of Whites. Come back!

– Paulin, I've brought you my photo. It's a testament to my love for you. Keep it in your room, during the entire time I'm away. Let me add a dedication: "To my darling Paulin, with my unchanging love. Sincerely, Marina." Take it and cherish it. As if it were me in person.

The room grows even darker. Paulin is bathed in sweat. She hasn't written to me in three months. She's given me no sign of life. Is it true what I've been told about her? Suddenly, Paulin feels what seem like exploding grenades in his head. At the base of his skull, a volcano roils, explodes. And the crater rips apart violently. Screaming of lava. Bottomless hole out of which giant flowers surge – monstrous and bloody.

– What's this? You're wearing a long white dress with a train. Marina! A thin man holds you by the arm . . . You're married! I see the lit candlesticks . . . I hear the hymns – the "Come, Creator Spirit!" . . . You're leaving the church on your husband's arm. And so it is that you've become someone else's wife. So this is how you betray our love?

Suddenly, a blinding flash surges from Paulin's eyes. His eyelids blink rapidly. He holds his head in his hands for a moment. Then picks it up. And sees the large signed photo of Marina back on its shelf. He's exhausted. For three months, not a day has gone by that he hasn't lived, in his thoughts, his sad love story. Imagining all the scenes of this unrequited love. Going over the painful path to failure. In an unbearable torture. In fact, it was happening just then to him . . . right after the departure of his friend Raynand, who'd looked at the photo. It had been three months since he'd learned of Marina's marriage in a foreign country. Three months . . .

After a few moments spent lost in bitter reflection, Paulin gets up. Wipes his brow. Rubs his head, inside of which wheels full of teeth seem to grind. Then says to himself that this is the last time . . . the last time.

– My obsession is over. Reason is now looking for a way past the fragility and weakness of the body. My nerves tense up in the face of the dust and the rust of the dreary darkness. A blaze burns inside me. My heart has jumped into my fiery mouth. I want my words to be embers. And if my voice drains all the blood clots, it's that my chest is ripening a glowing red apple tree in the place of my heart.

Tired out, Paulin moves toward the bookshelf. Picks up the photo. And places it carelessly in a corner. Far back in an old faded buffet. The corner of the forgotten. His complete healing.

■   ■   ■

In my native province, as a very young man, I learned from the peasants that one should never go to sleep on an empty stomach. Famished sleepers, they cautioned me, suffer the torments of a repose polluted by nightmares. I had the experience without intending to one night when I couldn't find anything to put in my mouth.

That night, I'd lain down in my bed earlier than usual, worn out by the day's labors. Sleep came quickly, despite my agitation. But what happened next, and must have been a nightmare, remains a troubling enigma for me to this day. On the margins of everyday life. Between dream and reality.

I was walking along a narrow street, accompanied by strange creatures. Monstrous. Handicapped. Having emerged from the factory of some demon counterfeiter. Let loose on the world without control. Spilled hurriedly onto the market of the living, their sole purpose being to consume. They were missing, respectively, some organ or the other. Their points of distinction. A whole range of hideous malformations. Faces pocked with holes. Without eyeballs. Heads without ears. Bodies without heads. Legless cripples. They spoke incessantly, yet seemed unable to understand one another. A surrealist game of automatic language. Dadaist Babel.

– Where have my madrepore eyes flown away to? I want to rinse the skin of sickly words in the humid air. My mouth opens and closes, entablature of star-laden branches. I'll trim the tapestries of the sky so as to bandage the wounds of light and the leprosy of the moon.

– I threw up my brains through my nostrils, in the form of a liqueur imbibed by birds of prey, lapped up by drunken dogs. I will detach my hollow head and use it in a volleyball match.

– I've buried my heart in a bottle and tossed it into the sea. The message insults the throne of kings and discredits the aqueous genitals of my mistresses. As a bee, I fly from tree to tree and peck at the young fruits.

– A voyager thirsting for space, I gather nectar and pollen and I become delirious from the perfume of the stars.

– My hair gives shelter to vermin. Let us raise the curtain of deception for the

backwash of lies. The jesters throw out the wash water. And the virgins chatter, touched by roaming tomcats who fart forcefully while opening their flies.

– Writer of prefaces for state-sponsored publications, I announce the disintegration of abandoned towns. I weigh the fleshy lips of the poets. I clean the mold off of animals and plants. I open the shutters of the clouds and throw the herb tea of the Assumption down the throats of drinkers of warm blood.

– Where have they gone, my feet and my arms, leaving me unable to run and embrace the girl being auctioned, and thus to try my luck against the prejudice of love? Without regret, I bet my pupils on the washed-out cheekbones of an anonymous cadaver.

– We live in the muck. From morning till night we empty out the mass graves, looking for the organs we're lacking. It's nothing but a waste of time. Everything gets mixed up and entangled under the piles of fallen rocks thrown at us by some intruder. We would do better, crippled companions, to seek out the guilty one and punish him. He's here. Hidden among us.

– Here's the intruder! The one who has never spoken. He's all in one piece, this one. He's been making fun of us. He's not missing any organs. Let us seize him. And distribute his parts to the mutilated. His ears. His eyes. His nose. His brain. His heart.

– Yes. Let us share his organs. Take him alive!

And all these pieces of humanity came closer to me. Pounced on me. Tied me up with intestines. I wanted to scream. I realized that I was mute and that my tongue was missing. So I tried to explain to them that I was missing an organ, that I'd been denied the use of language. But all my gestures were in vain. To convince them, I jumped up and down on my two feet. Then I opened my mouth wide. I woke up with a start in my own bed. Bathed in sweat. Out of breath. I got up wearily. After drinking a bit of cool water, I checked my watch for the time. Five in the morning. I reflected on the strangeness of my nightmare, which seemed to have lasted the entire night. Understanding nothing, I spoke about it with my friends that same day. My stupefaction was all the more troubling when it became clear that they'd all had the same nightmare, with only some slight variations. The agitated repose of famished sleepers, the peasants said to me whenever I spent my holiday in the provinces.

■　■　■

– How's it going, Raynand?
– My dear Paulin, things aren't going well at all. For some time now, everything has gotten complicated. A rise and fall that yields nothing. Even finding some grub has become an unsolvable problem.

That day, Raynand and Paulin meet outside Sylvio Cator Stadium. It's six in the evening. Paulin has just returned from a tutoring session he's been doing for the past month with two sons of a businessman from the Carrefour-Feuilles area. Raynand, for his part, has been walking for hours. He isn't even aware of how long it's been. He's always been a pair of legs walking. Bringing him nowhere. In the city. In the wind. From the earliest hours of the morning on, he begins his walk, contemplating the pale light of night's end. His secret joy, the conquest of dawn. It's then that the most rebellious stars fight not to disappear into the greedy mouth of the invading light in which the day sets up house. Inscribe a new page in the blue of the sky. A sweet ravishing. Surprising the sun's retractable claws as they scrape at the death throes of the night. Peeling back the mourning veil from all dead things. Destroy. Create. Change. Place oneself at the center of all movement. Transform oneself. Become the very hinge, the supreme core of movement. Get mixed up with the dust of atoms, essence of infinite vertigo. Immortality. Raynand has often told himself he'll never die. He knows it. He's convinced of it. And if it were to happen, his heart would lift up the earth. And out of it would emerge a flamboyant mango tree that would flower in the month of June. Flowers to decorate a great altar of repose, for the Corpus Christi. Benediction for the pair of shoes we're lacking! Benediction for our worn-out clothes! Benediction for our handicapped love stories! Benediction for the victims of assassination! Benediction for the blood of innocents!

Raynand begins walking very early in the morning. The last star is swallowed up. The road menders sweep the streets, clean the gutters, wash out the sewers, gather up the detritus in metallic wheelbarrows. All this, in his presence. Every day. Every morning.

Peeking over the flakes of white clouds, the sun immediately opens its heavy lids after a long sleep. It tears off the paralysis of the night. The trees quiver. Raynand perceives the slightest palpitations of the landscape and participates in all the stirrings of the day. Each time he'd imagine that something strange was going to happen; that the earth would capsize . . . That the balance would tip once and for all . . . That the planet would topple over . . . That the houses would collapse . . . That all beings and things would fly away, scattered – sucked up by the headwinds . . . His detached head would become a black moon . . . His dispersed limbs would light up, like so many incandescent cigars . . . Each time he left his house, he'd imagine that an extraordinary explosion would make the whole world blow up. But nothing out of the ordinary ever happened. Nothing came along to change the order of things. The days followed one another monotonously. Raynand seems condemned to repeat the same gestures, to hit his head against the stone walls and harshness of daily disappointments. Illusions. Dissatisfactions. What's more, he still hopes to be able to grab hold of that nodal point out of which all movement unfolds. That's the secret. The real discovery he's after. To seize movement by the throat. And to create the event!

From morning on, he walks without stopping. His sole and apparent freedom: walking. Although he often considers his meanderings to be nothing but a sham. A sort of open prison. A boxing in without motivation. An absurd environment. Because he can do nothing other than walk. He has no choice. He's needed nowhere. He passes unnoticed. The world functions well enough without him. He's nothing more than an appendix, like his brother, dead three years ago, struck down by a bullet at point-blank range. He was trying to cross the border to find work as a cane cutter in the Dominican Republic. The sentinel had cried, "Halt!" And off went the gunshot that had made no change to the course of history. Nor to the flow of rivers. The sun continued to rise in the East, to set in the West. Nothing had changed. Except that the next day, he'd had the overwhelming certainty of his brother's death. Fallen stone dead near the border. A bit of warm blood trickling from his mouth, a scarlet snake boldly emerging from its inconvenient hiding place. And then, the tears of an old mother. The bothersome words of people from the neighborhood, who, with a melancholy air, said, "Poor devil" when they heard the news. Nothing more than an appendix sliced off. Nothing more than a crushed ant. Nothing more than an earthworm torn to pieces.

Raynand walks all day long. Sometimes all night. He barely eats. A sort of ache, a rope sling made up of the tough strings of suffering, devours his entrails. Grains of sand roll about in his dry throat. Thousands of leeches drink his blood. Little by little, the pain in his stomach is joined by a strange army with spears that drill into his navel and pierce through his entire body. An invasion of open jaws. Masses of hooked teeth. He's reduced to a body of pain in motion. He no longer has any consciousness of the streets. So it is that one afternoon, at six o'clock, he runs into his friend Paulin and invites him to dinner, a dish of grilled pork and rice. At the little bar, Eugene's Place. South end of Sylvio Cator Stadium.

– You're not doing anything, Raynand.

– Absolutely nothing. For months now, I've got neither tobacco nor pipe. Neither dust nor smoke.

– For me, there isn't much going on either. But I'm getting by.

– What have you been doing, Paulin?

– I give private lessons to the children of this businessman over by Carrefour-Feuilles. That brings in about a hundred dollars a month. It isn't much. But I make do with that.

– Where I'm at right now, I'd make do with a quarter of that. And I've been looking. I've walked everywhere. Like a mad dog. I haven't found anything.

– Tell me, Raynand. If I remember correctly, you're from the Montrouis area?

– From Déluge, to be precise. But I have some relatives living in Montrouis. Farmers . . .

– Would you be able to make a little trip to the region?

– Why are you asking, Paulin?

– I'll let you know in a bit. For the time being, just answer me. I just want to help you out.

– How so? I don't see the connection.

– Do they grow groundnuts in the region?

– What are groundnuts?

– They're what we call pistachios around here.

– Paulin, you aren't about to ask me to sell grilled pistachios to get back on my feet.

– No. I just want to know if they grow pistachios in the region.

– You can find them on the neighboring mountains and in the hills around there. I remember seeing fields of pistachios the last time I was in Montrouis. In that scorched and rocky dirt. That was about seven years ago now. I think the pods germinate in the soil, which then has to be scratched and dug through when it's time for the harvest.

– Well, then. You'll be doing some scratching and digging, Raynand. You're going to root around in your head to make something come out.

– I don't understand – I don't get it, responds Raynand, eyes bulging.

– Just listen. The other day, the businessman whose kids I give lessons to was talking about a pretty interesting project, right in front of me. An American industrialist has come to the country to make an important deal. Apparently, he's already made contact with certain officials with an eye to pistachio farming.

– To what end?

– They're used to make oil and soap.

– Is it really a sure thing, Paulin? Because it'll take time to put together a soap or an oil factory. Setting up the business, the scrap iron, the installation of the machines. I'd have to wait too long.

– Not at all. The factory is already in place somewhere in the Caribbean. In Puerto Rico, I believe. A boat would come pick up the pistachios here in Haiti. The processing would happen over there.

– How much is this rich industrialist set to pay us for a sack of pistachios?

– I don't know yet. At the very least, it should be enough to get you back on your feet. I'm going to put you in contact with my friend, the businessman. He's in direct communication with the American. He won't say no, I'm sure of it. You, for your part, you'll sort out a warehouse.

– I'm up for it. I'll wait for the response. Then I'll make my way to Montrouis.

– It'll work, Raynand. You'll see.

– I hope so, with all my heart, Paulin. In any case, I thank you . . . Wait a second, Paulin. And the title of your novel?

– Haven't yet figured it out, Raynand. But it'll come to me on its own. In fact, you'd be doing me an immense favor if you'd suggest a title for me.

■ ■ ■

Raynand has been in Montrouis for the past week. From the moment of his arrival, he'd made arrangements with Verdieu Belhomme to procure a certain amount of pistachios, about the equivalent of a hundred bags.

Once upon a time, Verdieu Belhomme had been a perfectly gallant farmer. Today, he's nothing more than a shadow of himself. His first son left him to live a dissolute life in the capital. His wife died that same year. His daughter Célie, a beautiful girl, it's said, also abandoned him. She packed her things one morning and hopped on the first big truck that went by. Since then, she lives as a prostitute in a brothel in Port-au-Prince, the Royal-Cabaret, where's she's all the rage.

Verdieu Belhomme rarely leaves his village. He no longer goes to the capital – it's been at least ten years. He's resigned to his life as a field rat. Not hoping for anything better. Just waiting for death. He often regrets his naïveté at having listened to that white preacher who'd advised him to get married. To have only one wife, in accordance with the laws of God and Christian morality. He'd stupidly obeyed the preacher, who knew absolutely nothing about this strange land of Haiti. Who didn't understand that the strategy of the Haitian peasant is to take as many mistresses or wives as possible to produce multiple clutches of children for him. The great law of accumulation that underlies the rural economy of the family. The supreme solution to the problem of a sufficient workforce. Verdieu Belhomme often asks himself how he'd been so foolish as to break that fundamental law of the Haitian peasantry, and to follow the treacherous advice of that preacher, who left him in a state of misery and confusion. He wouldn't have ended up where he is today – as a disgraced peasant. He'd be like his neighbor Chérilus, a King Midas with the Golden Touch, with his thirty-seven children. Ah! Children! The wealth of the poor. Sure support for old age.

Today, he's all alone. Denim pants with holes in the seat in the shape of two hexagonal eyes. A shirt so shredded that it's as if it had been saved at the last minute from the jaws of a raging bull. Long, thin machete on his right hip. Downcast visage that makes him look older than his fifty years. Verdieu Belhomme walks against the wind, on every pathway, over all the hills of Montrouis, which he knows by heart, just as he knows the dry and rainy seasons of the year.

For some time now, happiness has been elusive. When he goes to or returns from his cursed garden, he looks just like a fighting cock. Beak to the ground. Disconcerted. Bruised by strikes of multiple spurs. Ow! Such stubborn soil! So many trials for one human being! This life, even tougher and heavier than carrying a casket on one's head. The sterile soil, an old menopausal woman. When he drinks his rum, his fingers tremble, his lips twist into a bitter grimace. Such terrible luck! A narrow passageway holds back his limbs. The wrong paths break his momentum. It's as if an invisible machine is chewing up his life like stalks of cane in a mill. The gears tighten. But he's left with neither juice nor molasses. He thinks, with regret, that for a long while now he's been reduced to a pile of old, dried-up cane stalks, good for burning to repel mosquitoes. His life: ridiculous. Insignificant as that mesquite tree, tilted toward its fatal decline. Covered in moss, a hairy beard. He's no longer a beautiful tall tree. His flesh, torn apart by blows of the ax. His mouth, crushed. His gums, toothless. His body, laced with scars. Tripped up and tumbling over. Running into tree stumps. His vision barely reaches over the hedge of candelabra cacti that border his little *ajoupa*. His activities end at the enclosure of his garden, his everyday landscape. Misery on his heels, faithful companion. The desolation corseting his hips in barbed wire. Distress down to the very roots of his being.

Despite everything, Verdieu Belhomme still knows how to get unstuck. To sort himself out so as not to die too quickly. He manages to find a pretty good stock of pistachios for Raynand.

– And the money – when do you think you'll have it? he asks Raynand.

– As soon as the boat comes to pick up the first loads of pistachios. Maybe in about two weeks.

– You're sure we can trust this American's word? says Verdieu Belhomme skeptically.

– Don't worry. The American will send the boat. With the money, of course. He's a rich man. He seems to really need these pistachios for his soap and oil factory in Puerto Rico.

– All the same, let's wait. We're really counting on this deal.

– It'll work. There's no doubt.

– You're not thinking that it's the Good Lord of the poor who's come to help us in the form of some white man. That's not it, is it, Raynand?

Raynand doesn't answer. The next day, he returns to Port-au-Prince with his load of pistachios and puts them in an old house on Saint-Martin Street. Waiting for the steamer *Mary-Jane*.

■   ■   ■

More than a month goes by. The *Mary-Jane* still hasn't pulled into the harbor in Port-au-Prince. Day and night, Raynand walks in circles down at the wharf. In the beginning, visions of bundles of dollar bills danced in his head. He whistled happily from morning to night, humming boleros, rancheras, and all sorts of popular tunes. He'd fall asleep and plunge into a dream of future projects, at the end of which there was always a little car, a pretty house. And, of course, all of his beautiful dreams featured the presence and the finery of an imaginary woman, a marvelous spouse who'd make Solange regret her betrayal.

Some weeks later, he started feeling nervous. An interminable waiting game. Rain falling every night. Unbearably hot days. A sniggering sun, a veritable fire monster. A fire-breathing dragon. And then, in the afternoon, the dry earth split open, becoming chapped. And the next night, rain. A veritable *tolalito* – a hopeless quest – set to the rhythm of downpours and relentless sun. A constant *maïs-l'or*,* livened up at times by a slow-turning game of jump rope with either the sun or the moon.

After a month of fruitless waiting, Raynand is devastated to learn that the American was an impostor. A fake industrialist. He'd figured out how to exploit the situation of underdeveloped countries so as to mint money. A crafty bugger who'd put his mind to work at thieving and scheming. He'd been to several islands of the Caribbean where he'd been able to collect

---

* Children's game that consists of pivoting around and around on one foot.

immense sums with a mere signature. A white man's initials – that's a guarantee! In poor Haiti, he'd managed to squeeze more than a hundred thousand dollars out of his naïve partners. Not to mention the awful trick he'd pulled on those who'd stocked enormous quantities of unsold pistachios.

Overcome, Raynand listens to Paulin tell him about the numerous exploits of this international con man, a thieving artist, a Luciferian monster vomited up by the hell of a decadent American society. Evidence, also, of the naïveté and innocence of the world's little people. But now, there'd never be a boat, Raynand says to himself. Pulling himself together, he leaves Paulin. He heads directly toward the old house on Saint-Martin Street, where he'd stored his sacks of pistachios. What would he do with them? He doesn't really know. But he's worried about what to tell Verdieu Belhomme. For the time being, the main thing would be to save some part of the money by reselling the pistachios on the cheap.

This morning, the weather is just fine. The temperature cool. The sun shines without heating things up too much. The sky a clear blue. Cloudless. The key to the warehouse in his right hand, Raynand begins to think, maybe even to dream. Seated on the narrow concrete-coated step leading up to the depot.

＊　＊　＊

Far away. He falls into a moment of total distraction during which a series of confused images follow one another incoherently. Without paying any particular attention, he crushes all the little ants swarming up his splayed legs. A cockroach passes by and he flattens it with a quick jab of his heel.

A sticky, whitish substance surges from the insect's rear, and he looks at it for a while. Hideous creature, I crushed your foundations, your vile parachute. You won't do any more damage. Go back to the malodorous gutter you came from. Life is already so difficult. Man can't even feed himself. There's not the slightest piece of straw to spare for parasitic beasts. The tender flesh of cats is edible. The drunkards know that all too well. It's time, long past time that we start eating dogs and rats. Raynand scratches at the dusty ground with the tip of his shoe, covering over the roach, which clearly isn't completely dead, as its legs are still moving. How to escape, when life is nothing more than a brief parenthesis in the interminable dictation of absences and death? And Man is no good at spelling. The centuries, a long series of exterminations. Raynand ends up burying the insect under clumps of earth. What a marvelous grave digger I'd make! he says to himself, standing up. He fits the key into the lock. He turns it twice to the left. The double doors open instantly onto a marvelous burst of colored wings. An awakening of wriggling, unexpected light. A multicolored flight of butterflies whip Raynand's face. Confetti of noisy wings. A gentle rain of butterflies – purple, blue, yellow, sequined, striped with black luminescence, green phosphorescence. A swarming, sparkling kaleidoscope.

On the damp floor, piles of blond caterpillars. No more pistachios. All that's left are a few rotten pods in the humidity of the room. More than half the stock had flown off in a fireworks of wings and luminous dust. Raynand doesn't even try to understand. What would he know about the marvelous process of metamorphosis? How would he ever be able to seize, in flight and on the fly, the brilliant rainbow in which animal and vegetable meet in all their splendor on a bridge of softness and clarity? And so he prefers to distance himself from the shock of this shack. Without saying a word. Nourishing the blissful illusion that he'd been the maker of miracles in the middle of the day.

In traversing the entry gate, he surprises himself by thinking, without really knowing why, about Paulin's novel – still without a title.

■ ■ ■

Daughter, bring me a straw chair so I can sit down! The hard rock is hurting my bottom. And I'm tired from standing up for so long. I want to gaze upon the teats of time. The jumble of clouds eaten away by parasites. The moon secretes a sour milk on stubborn eyes. Inflamed gaze from the burns of corrosive stars. My daughter is a child of the islands where a people of sleeping warriors reside. Fever of the past. Coldness of the present. Uncertainty of the future. The chained-up giants fear their own awakening. Phobia of risk. Tired spines. Death is up on its feet. Let's lay it down in a hammock and rock it to sleep! Combat ruse and not pitiful surrender. My daughter is from Haiti. Island with gaping jaws. What troubling expectation is being incubated at its black breasts? Mountainous island with its marrow sucked dry by foreign lions.

Daughter, bring me a low chair so I can stretch out on the arbor of old stories from back home. The dying wizard cannot take the whole village to the cemetery with him, says the old man with the white beard. The tale is so long that the end won't come soon enough. Patience is a slow team of oxen in the night. May my eldest daughter serve white rum to the neighbors who come to take part in the exorcism of the castle steeped in a nightmare! Set up the chairs in a circle and leave a place in the center for the best storyteller to animate the wake. He speaks. The chorus responds: if ever the earth should tremble, may the children of tender and pure flesh survive!

Nathalie, my daughter, listen well . . . Once upon a time there was a giant with unusually long fingers. Fingers that crossed mountains, oceans, continents. Swept away the plains. Stirred up the sea. Rooted around in the soil. Took away the cattle, the provisions, the precious metals. This clever giant thus took over all the useful things that do not belong to him. Seized all goods to be found within ten thousand leagues of his home. And with his powerful fingers he even uprooted the living, grabbing them by the stomach. Insatiable, he drank the blood of all living beings. Inexorably he chewed up the bones of any valiant warriors who dared to protest.

With time, the giant got old, and even more cruel. But the men remained undaunted. They waited. Hoped. Watched. Prepared their revenge. The great trap . . . One night, while the monster slept, they lit great wood fires. In the mountains. In the islands. Everywhere. The flames rose up to the sky in a pure yellow. Awakening with a start, the giant, whose vision had weakened with age, thought that some new sources of gold, oil, and petroleum had emerged from the earth. Without losing any time, he plunged his long fingers in deeply . . . Fateful error! He let loose a long and horrible scream. A death wail that shook up all living things. First his fingers, then his arms scorched to the elbows. Given that he was detested in his own home by his subjects, he was finished off quickly. Ferociously. And with the fatty flesh of his body, the overjoyed people made firecrackers and torchlight tattoos. Torches of fraternal reconciliation. Of friendship. Of true love. Which exploded in a hail of stars and fires of joy.

With the change in weather, the drummers and the sambas of the new season sing, and so proclaim a future tale: there will sometime be . . .
One time, a little girl with a triangular chin, in love with a blue bird . . .
Ah! Nathalie, my child, your father is so jealous!

■   ■   ■

Each new day brings with it a truckload of worries. Old wheelbarrow of suffering. More and more, Raynand feels as if he's been secured to a paralytic's stretcher. And no longer has control of his legs in the sand-blocked bitterness of dead ends. His arms only know how to carry the hideous box of endless bad luck on the paths of sorrow. How would he ever manage to clear out such stony earth with a strike of the shovel? To hollow out the hard and compact granite with a strike of the pickax? To break apart my convict's chains? My skull, trapped in a steel girdle, shelters a devastating nightmare. It's crucial that I unbind the rope of my inner pain. That I exorcise the demon that resides in each one of us. On my interminable path I've already crossed too many sickos. Lovers of vice, pedophiles, impostors, mass murderers, con artists, lesbians, adulterers, alcoholics, drug addicts, mentally ill, wanton liars, impenitent criminals – they all crawl out of their lairs. They shuffle around, masks lifted. Deploy their dark banner against a rusty sun. Carry the sacrament under the richly adorned canopy of imperial audacity, arrogance, and impunity.

Absent any revolutionary salvation, there's only anarchy left capable of striking the most furious blow on the demoniacal fortress. I'm waiting for the savior to come. The avenging Christ will unload his stock of violent poisons into the streams, the rivers, the cisterns. I've already begun laughing at all those people who walk around the streets not knowing they're all going to die, one after the next. They don't realize that their security is nothing but an illusion, that the whole town could disappear in one day if, in a single punitive act, the lord of anarchy were to unleash his cargo of violent poisons into their drinking water. Let him come, the god of popular vengeance for the redemption and the salvation of the world! Then the restaurants, the bars, the hotels, all kitchens would serve nothing but poisoned dishes. The prostitutes would shoot off the cocks of all the flesh peddlers, magnificent celebration in honor of sex. The hairdressers and the barbers, discovering the violent power of their razor blades, would slit their clients' throats. Oh, blessed exterminating bombs! The vastness of pain salutes you on the highest pinnacle of the planet. Bloody genuflection in death's kitchen. Let the flames of terror shine! Let the total revolution explode so that the universe might be cleansed of all its rottenness and all its pestilence!

However, accompanied by the angel of suicide, I would make a majestic bid for immortality. But the sea in which I try to drown myself freezes up. Blind mirror that reflects my ugliness back to me. The blade I pass across my throat doesn't cut. Becomes a bow that extracts nothing more from me – sexless violin – than a parody of sound. The stiletto, with which I'd pierce my heart, breaks against my chest of dead stone. All firearms jam as soon as they're turned on me. I'm courting eternity by way of suicide. I attain the sainted purity of the devil. I'd like to throw myself off the top of some edifice. Be crushed against the hard ground. Star-shaped bloody splashes. But I'm as light as a feather. Swallow a dose of arsenic – my stomach rejects it. Hang myself – all the ropes are already rotting away. Slash my arteries – my blood coagulates. Throw myself under the wheels of a train – the spiral of its speed whisks me away.

So goes Raynand, a locomotive of despair, life nipping at his heels. Death doesn't leave us free to choose it. To hold it tight. To wed oneself to it. The thing is, it only knows how to give traitorous kisses. Suicide, sacred tabernacle, proves difficult to access for the conscious being. All flight, impossible. Only the trials of intolerable days and nights. Purgatory, in which total atonement bleaches one's bones.

And Raynand, tired of walking endlessly and without any objective, becomes an incessantly speaking mouth. The suffering flesh becomes word through my voice. I sniff out the yapping of dogs perched atop the peak of a flaming bonfire. Castrated soldiers carry rusty rifles. No transit for the merry-go-round. Paradise lost. Man lies crippled in a space under surveillance, where anarchic violence reigns. Counterfeit freedom. The barycenter shifts epileptically with every second. Scalp the leprous skin and cauterize the wound with vitriol. At the midday tribunal, Saint Nicholas judges the criminals, the murderers, and the masters of power waiting at the construction site of evil. A generation of epileptics gushes out. No more muzzles! No more straitjackets! No more! . . .

Raynand walks. Talks. He doesn't only talk from his mouth. His entire body traces the triumphant space of the forbidden word. Ostracism or communion in the suffocation of the word. He walks. When he arrives at Paulin's house, the latter is busy writing a chapter of his novel.

– Still no title, Paulin?

– The title is a fiery scab that I leave for the cover. For the skin of my work.

– You know, Paulin, I've been at the end of my rope for a long time. Over and over I'm brought to consider the gratuitousness of my little drama, the uselessness of my existence. If I were a writer like you, if I were working on a novel, I'd make it so that each printed page inspired the taking up of arms. The sad thing is that since my childhood I've been living as if pursued by a pack of rabid dogs. In a locked enclosure. Without any openings in the fence. A recluse, I wonder if my life has done nothing but ferment decay, vermin, and rotting carcasses from one end to the other. And I've come to the conclusion that I amount to nothing more than the suppurations of some malodorous fate.

– Raynand, you're heading backward. You're caught up in yourself. And you seem to be saying: look how I'm suffering. Raynand, never attract the compassion of others. Despise the pity of others.

– Paulin, what do you know of my troubles? What do you know about my problems and the drama of waiting for someone to throw me a rope?

– But, Raynand, everyone has problems. I have them, too. I've long been living out the tribulations of my childhood. Have I ever told you the story?

– Go ahead, I'm listening.

– Yes, we all have our problems. I often imagine the conversation that could take place between myself and Death. Between Death, in its macabre attire, and me, dying in my bed. Between Death, with its cursed mouth, and the dying man I already am.

◼ ◼ ◼

Dying Man: I haven't even finished my day and here you are calling for me. All these unfinished tasks and aborted dreams I'll leave behind me!

Death: Don't worry yourself over such small things. It's time for you to rest. After so many years on stage. Life is a theater in the round where the actors remain standing. For the entire time. Since the curtain never lowers, it's quite a responsibility I've taken on – making exhausted actors lie down.

Dying Man: No. I'm far from exhausted. I've still got plenty of lines on the tip of my tongue. Let me get in a few more tirades. And then I'll retire my role.

Death: Alas! It's far too late for that. What have you done with your life, from your birth to this day . . . pitiful mortal?

Dying Man: I've been looking for myself.

Death: Did you find yourself?

Dying Man: Life slipped through my fingers. I was never able to get ahold of it.

Death: Because you only ever thought of yourself. Because others didn't exist for you. Say! What happened to your friends? Your parents?

Dying Man: My parents are dead.

Death: I know.

Dying Man: My defunct mother, a naïve peasant impregnated by my defunct father. A rich industrialist. Possessed by the demon of eroticism. Violently subjugated by sexual passion. A misogynist of the worst order, he always said, in true macho style, that all women are females. He got into the pants of half a dozen every day.

Death: Sad record!

Dying Man: That was his battlefield. His field of honor. His personal war. His sickness. His favorite game – until that fatal heart attack. He died of it one night. Having left this earth voluptuously in a final burst of sperm.

Death: Glory be to him, that valiant cavalier of horizontal confrontations!

Dying Man: Well before his death, he'd stopped taking care of me. I grew up quickly. Torn between the pity I felt for my mother and the hatred I felt for everyone else around me. The taste for solitude took root in me.

Death: But solitude is no more than an escape. Vain flight. Often an impasse.

Dying Man: Yet I never gave up the fight. To get out of the impasse was the challenge I'd given to myself.

Death: You were too attached to your unhappy past. Did you ever break the infernal circle of the "I" in order to enter into the luminous round that is the "we?" Did you for even one day try to break through the triangle of limitation? Did you really acknowledge your weaknesses? What have you done with your life?

Dying Man: My whole life I've owned up to both my strengths and my weaknesses. I've never claimed to be an angel. Nor a saint either. I was born in the dust of an uncertain dawn. Obstacles, unexpectedness, spontaneity, pain, bursts of sorrow and joy fill my travel journal from my long journey to unknown lands.

Death: You never knew the itinerary. You didn't even make an effort to figure out the point of the journey.

Dying Man: I tried. Looked. Stumbled. The journey is peopled with nightmares. Each time I glimpse the light, a wave of mist rises up. A thick fog immediately covers my eyelids. And then, fearing exile on the edge of this darkness, I run tirelessly into closed doors. Barely does a bit of light begin to flutter than the breath of evil snuffs out all hope at its roots.

Death: So you give up, having neither the courage nor the patience to handle impossibility during difficult times. What would you do if I left and didn't take you? How would you choose to live the newest scenes of this great drama?

Dying Man: I wouldn't hesitate. I would still choose to be a man. And not a saint. I would be reborn with the same weaknesses. I would make the same mistakes that led to me remaining a man – that is, a being who seeks himself in the cries of blood in the darkness.

Eyes wild, and inspired by Paulin's feverishly related imaginary dialogue, Raynand presses him further:

– Paulin, I think that's all you need to put in your work. Write a novel drawn from the fodder of your own life. And that just might end up being worth something. Because it will be the lived history of a man. Sending out a luminous band into the night while waiting to discover the very heart of the day. Moving from the differential to the integral. That's the miracle you could achieve in using the most central facts of your own life.

– You've got that absolutely right, Raynand. In the tracing of the spiral, I've written pages that recall somehow the journal of a traveler who's set off to follow a series of overlapping and fleeting paths.

– How so? Tell me what you mean.

– These pages, despite their autobiographical nature, distinguish themselves from a private journal. They're not burdened by any chronology. They're more like a tangled film. The fuzzy cinema of certain key events of my life. In these pages, the essential for me was to give free rein to my imagination as it rides memories that, paradoxically, belong at once to the past, the present, and even prolong my life into a formless future. Spiralist writing mixes up time and space. It's an aesthetic approach that emerges from both relativity and quantum theory.

– This sounds like a promising experience – one that I'd like to follow closely. Would you allow me to read a few pages?

– I have no objection to that. I'll give them to you right now, if you'd like. You can read them this evening, at your place. These pages are poetic, written in the style of the Total Genre. The Spiralist genre, which embraces at once the novel, poetry, the folktale, theater . . . In an impressive liaison. The whole thing harmonized in a single architectural ensemble. In order to reconcile art and life.

– Okay, you can give me a few pages. I'll read them tonight.

Paulin gets up from his worktable. He opens the right-hand drawer of a pine desk and takes out a stack of marked-up papers to give to Raynand.

■   ■   ■

Back in his modest room, Raynand readies himself to read the pages Paulin has written. Ten o'clock. The night is calm. So he'll be able to read without being disturbed. Savoring the first lines, he lights a cigarette. As he reads, fragments of thoughts and images emerge. Form arabesques. Then disappear. With certain passages, an entire inner world opens up. A world that's nearly ungraspable. Pure cry. Poetic vision. Will-o'-the-wisps of a fermenting brain. Is the point to try and capture some glimmer? One would have to use a new writing technique, then – one capable of following the uneven and intermittent unfolding of the inner panorama. And of capturing the concentric ideas, the parallel or divergent beams, the vanishing waves. A sort of quest within the subconscious that would call for the sheet of paper to be split into two columns: on the left, the writer's text; on the right, in the form of annotations, the resonances provoked in the reader. Or better still, the left page would be used for the bursts of writing of a fictional nature. And the right page would be for the whirling of the interior monologue and the subtext.

■   ■   ■

How and when am I going to die? Moment of contact with the hereafter. Crime doesn't take the weekend off. It takes a lot more effort to come back from a bad dream than to get tangled up in sleep. Forgetting. Branch by branch. Stone by stone. Flesh bitten by the knife. Strike of fangs. Spurting of fresh blood. Liquefaction happens incessantly. I become an accomplice to the wind that separates out the dirt and the poisonous fillings.

It is urgent that we capture the escaped python. Allow it to slip – alive – around our neck. Unstoppably talkative, my soul radiates the stripes of time on the paleness of the autumn landscape.

Friendship loses water from the torn basket, which retains only the brackish mud. Where have they all gone, the friends I loved so dearly?

The wind is better than I am at finding the feeble spark that will keep reddening independent of the scattered ashes.

Again, I make the mechanical gesture that reanimates my heart: a semblance of living.

The pure ones have never seen the sun set; they know nothing of the darkness or the veiled trickery of fog.

Who will dig out the center of marooning words? I'm talking about sugar granulated like the sex organs of a half-deflowered maiden. And I'd bet that there's no woman sweeter than the one you mount at dawn.

Have we captured the receiver of stolen goods from armed robberies? I hear the rumbling of drums all over the world. The devilment of Carnival rope launchers. Display of vampire wings. America spits red into the Mississippi. Let the valiant Negroes hold on to the password!

Near the terrace, I gesture to the girls carrying water, who instantaneously become paralyzed, blind, and mute. The calabashes are broken; I remain beside myself with thirst. Ah! Cactus-armed women, why do you turn me into a wandering ghost? Kill my fervor, suppress my hunger before you leave. The sun tilted toward the sea lays down my fleeting shadow. What bloody kiss will be able to freeze my lipless lover's heart?

It's always despicable that sand and water betray the secret fragility of love.

I appeal to torrential loves . . . plaintive washerwomen of the most squalid roadways!

Paper river mouth you sad suitcase stamp dead rock tobacco voice face agreement demand madness denial homeland fatigue love leaving work break misery rage race or flight ah! polyvalent life words men things stuffed with meaning! It's in you that I've searched for myself for so long and am still searching.

*   *   *

The small van, a Peugeot 404, cream colored, full to bursting, tears up the highway to Delmas. Among the passengers, Raynand and Paulin. Seated in the last row, they talk without stopping. The vehicle's speed seems to rip up the bushes, the electric poles, the pedestrians, the sidewalks. At the wheel of the car, Titon spiritedly executes his job as driver. He has to make the Port-au-Prince to Pétionville round-trip as quickly as possible. Finish off the day with a profit. Speed is the rule of the day. Accelerate. Win the race against time that flies and flies away. Go. Come back. Charge down the road. Speed. Drive. Devour the kilometers.

A passenger worries about the speed. You're going much too fast, she says.

Titon is a good driver. He knows his job. He's a real champion, responds Raynand.

A driver after my own heart! Faster than the wind! The open road beckons him to pounce. Faster than the wind! adds Paulin.

They attract the disapproving glances of the other passengers.

He who goes slowly arrives surely, replies an older man who hadn't said anything up to that point.

Ironic, euphoric, Paulin and Raynand flatter Titon's pride. They laud his agility in having just missed a mule crossing the road. Then, with an explosion of bawdy joy that shocks their neighbors, they take up and repeat:

Cherished driver, who knows how to heat things up! Go ahead and floor it! Dismantle your pedals! And smash right through death's asshole!

At the end of the line, near the Pétionville cemetery, a place that serves as a station for transport vans, Raynand and Paulin are last to get off. Reluctantly, they've come to attend the religious ceremony for Bob's wedding. They're really only interested in the reception, which follows the blessing. A nice way to spend a couple of hours. When they arrive, the godfather is just in the middle of making a toast to the new couple. A long line of cars are parked in front of the house. A gathering of the curious. Inside, the folkloric lighting is overwhelmingly blinding. Starving guests. Thirsty alcoholics. Pockets of silence. Whispers. Coughs. Commentaries spoken into one another's ears. The guttural and trembling voice of the orating godfather dominates the room with a false eloquence. Moldy speech. Scent of mothballs.

. . . like two inseparable turtledoves. My dear godchildren, you may experience difficult and trying moments. And it is then that you must really come together. In sincere and lasting dialogue, free of all secrets. Dialogue is the most eloquent form of mutual understanding. A union that rests on . . .

– Bob's wife seems very old. She's got to be more than forty.
– She's forty-three.
– Christ's age plus ten. An old she-devil with sawed-off horns. A real cradle robber! A complete fraud of a woman!
– She's rich. A well-stocked shop. A property in Laboule. Several cars. A fat bank account.
– Bob has bet it all on the ball that rolls around in the fat of dollar bills.
– Because two poor people combined still won't have enough to make ends meet . . .

. . . for happiness comes from inner peace. Material suffering doesn't kill conjugal life. It's the drying up of the soul that brings about rupture and ruin.

– The godfather is an out-and-out liar. Misery is the execution post of love.

. . . to acknowledge your duties to society, to the children you'll have to raise. For these things, fidelity is the key element . . .

– You think she can have kids?
– She's already well past her prime.
– A real tacky woman. Bitter and unripe.
– For a long time, she was the favorite mistress of a top customs employee who let her order her goods without paying any import tax.
– A real womanizer.

. . . to affirm, without risk of being contradicted, along with the eminent sociologist Frédéric Le Play, that the family is a social unit of the greatest importance. My dear godchildren, the commitment you've just made belongs to the purest humanist tradition. Christian Humanism, as defined by Saint Augustine in his remarkable work *The City of God*. If you understand that . . .

– He's boring us stiff with this endless funeral oration.
– It stinks of bad medicine and rotten fish.
– I'm tired of his verbal diarrhea.
– I'm thirsty. I'm hungry.
– My feet are killing me.

Impatience is written on everyone's face. People inhale the aroma from the champagne glasses. Standing, the guests keep shifting their weight. The neighborhood dogs bark incessantly. The waitresses and the kid who chops the ice bicker in the kitchen. And when, in the midst of some flight of lyricism crafted three months earlier especially for the end of his toast, the godfather invites all in attendance to empty their glasses in celebration of the newlyweds, a sigh of relief seems to escape from every chest, in a unanimous rush to do so.

Then the godmother, inviting the guests to the decorated tables, decides to take the floor, offering in turn some words of thanks. The majority of the guests stay up in front, some put the weight on their left foot, others on their right. Ready to go. In a likely race to the buffet. A frightening marathon of *aloufas* – so many greedy dogs – ready to pounce on the booty. Raynand already has his eyes fixed on an enormous pink cake. Strange swaying of torsos tilted forward for a final assault. Curious momentum of racers waiting for the starting whistle to blow. Jostling of elbows on a makeshift track where the finish line whets the appetite. Mouths water. With the godmother's final words, a powerful cyclone of open hands comes down on the decorated tables, mercilessly and neatly razed by hundreds of greedy fingers.

After this demoniacal Olympic storm, the guests, scattered into little groups, enjoy the drinks. The young girls and women drink Coca-Cola. The gentlemen drink unlimited quantities of whiskey or Barbancourt rum. The room is immediately transformed into picturesque fairgrounds. Exhibition of colorful moths. Farcical ostentation. Parade of miniskirts.

Disjointed comments marked by a touch of sophistication. Raynand and Paulin, seated at a strategic angle, attentively watch this high-society spectacle. Taking neat shots, they empty a half bottle of rum placed on a round table. Quietly, they exchange commentaries and gossip. They observe everything rigorously. From one thing to the next and without missing a beat.

∎ ∎ ∎

A short distance away, three elegantly dressed women chat and giggle together. They're soon joined by an impeccably ugly fourth woman, who's accompanied by a pretty young girl. The woman's face is dried up, eroded. An absurdly long neck. She's so hideous, she wouldn't be out of place among a collection of barn owls in a museum of horrors. A fluffed-up chicken. Exaggeratedly exuberant. Her talkativeness and tinny laugh irritate. With her skinny, jittery body, she recalls the jerking movements of a broom. An unbearable talking weather vane.

– My son Patrick took a trip last month. He's in the United States. He's doing his military service.

– You're not worried he'll be sent to the front in Vietnam?

– It's certainly a possibility. He's not planning on returning to Haiti. In fact, I encouraged him not to. What's important is that he secure a foothold over there. That brings certain advantages. He'll be able to open a path for us to the great industrial cities. In no short time, the whole family will settle in New York. I couldn't have hoped for better. Here, life has become impossible. A veritable hell on earth.

Raynand follows the conversation attentively. He touches Paulin's right knee.

– Paulin, do you know that woman?

– She's a lesbian. The pretty young girl with her is her official mistress.

– Is that really true?

– And, in fact, Raynand, the other ones are no better. They're corrupt politicians. Secret agents for foreign powers. Their husbands – a bunch of cowards. Freeloading assholes. Pedophiles. Smugglers. A real debauched crowd. In favor during the American Occupation, now ousted from the halls of power, they actually miss the Yankees. Since the white man can't come back and run the country, they all head over there to keep the old love story alive. So their good-for-nothing kiddies quit school before ever even studying the humanities and leave for the States. The most talented of the bunch study electronics, diesel mechanics, or business. The mediocre ones become dishwashers, dog groomers in New York, or cannon fodder in Vietnam. The people, filled with complexes, blinded by color prejudice, are only too happy to see their daughters married to some cowboy or gringo from Texas. They see it as a true godsend, manna from heaven. All of them flee Haiti, which, in their spite and resentment, they see as no more than savage-filled bush country. Bitter farewell to the good old days at the Club, where any black person who dared come in was looked upon disdainfully like a dirty black fly in a glass of milk. That's all gone for good!

Pensively, Raynand takes a drink, draws exaggeratedly on his cigarette. Paulin, eyes shining, head resting against a sign, continues talking. With his resonant voice. Passionate. A convincing tone that, in its fluctuations, manages to find just the right way into the heart or the mind. An empathetic understanding, without artifice or oversensitivity. A flood of emotions, but without flashy hysterics or embittered violence. A strong temperament, neither tough nor dogmatic. In short, a striking sensitivity. A generous connection. An elevating glimmer.

The contents of the bottle have diminished noticeably. Raynand, slightly tipsy, looks vaguely around at the crowd of attendees. A long-limbed gentleman walking across the salon toward the exit notices Paulin. He stops suddenly. Smilingly, he approaches the table:

– Good old Paulin, how the hell are you?

– Hanging in there. Raynand, meet my buddy Roger Drouillard, a friend from way back. He's a good guy. An intern at the medical college.

They clasp hands. Raynand, somewhat distant, doesn't catch the name of the young doctor, who makes no attempt to hide his pleasure at having run into Paulin at the reception.

– Well then, Roger, hang out with us for a bit. It's only nine o'clock. We'll get out of here around ten.

– Okay, Paulin, I was going to leave. But seeing you, I've changed my mind. An hour shooting the breeze with you sounds good to me. It's been so long since we last saw each other.

– Yeah, it's been a while.

– So what about that novel of yours? I've got to believe you're going to finish it this year. What title did you come up with?

– Still no title. In the end, I think I'll leave it up to Raynand to give it a title once I've finished it. This novel is a curse. It just won't let me rest.

– That's a good sign, an anxious creative process. Isn't that true, Paulin?

– More or less . . . And you, Roger, what have you been up to? Anything good?

– Fully mired in work at the hospital. This month I'm working the toughest, most exhausting service: the dispensary. Almost no sleep. You've got to stay up all night, on call for the unexpected.

– Do you ever have the day shift?

– Of course. There's plenty of turnover. We're on rotation. But it's still hard. For example, yesterday I worked from six in the morning to six at night. And I had a pretty tough day because of something of a strange case.

– What happened?

– It was about ten in the morning. A patient in his fifties shows up with a referral. Pale face. Glassy eyes. Shriveled-up shoes. Clothes full of patches, but well ironed. I was pretty sure those were his best clothes. I gave him my full attention, asking him methodically to give me all the information on the onset of an illness he claimed to be suffering from. Weakly, he explained to me that he'd been feeling a shooting pain in his back. He coughed at night. He barely ever slept. The thing is, he said, if this keeps up I could lose my job. Doctor, I can't be unemployed again, he implored; I can't afford to take to my bed; do something for me, and the good Lord will reward you a hundredfold. He explained to me that he'd worked as a road mender for the past twenty years. I had him lie down so as to check him out with my stethoscope. What I found horrified me. We're not talking about a death rattle. It was an absolute pulmonary cyclone. A real thoracic storm. With every breath, veritable blasts traversed the poor man's pulmonary alveoli, which had been largely replaced by innumerable caverns. In my ears, it was like violent gusts of wind in what was left of his lungs, irreparably eaten away by tuberculosis. He stayed lying down. I did my best to reassure him. I was going to hospitalize him. He thanked me with a limpid smile that moved me deeply. I left for a few minutes and came back with some hospitalization forms so that he might take advantage of a stay in a sanatorium. When I came back into the little room, I told him that it had worked, that we'd take care of him. He didn't answer. I went closer to the exam table. Harrowing shock. In my brief absence, the poor road mender had already died.

Roger is quiet for a moment. He fills his glass and continues his story.

– I was upset for the rest of the day.

– I understand you, brother, says Paulin.

– I'd just become aware of the tragic reality of intolerable injustices. I discovered the deplorable absurdity of life. That of a man who'd spent twenty years cleaning. Scrubbing. Sweeping. Keeping the city clean. And he'd just passed away. Like the dirty water he'd pushed along with his broom. Sidewalks with smelly sewers. For twenty years, he'd done nothing else. His whole life, for that matter. And here it was that his breath had been snuffed out in the great void of his destroyed lungs. It was then that I understood the meaning of his limpid smile when he thanked me. For the first time in his existence as a brute laborer he'd found someone to take care of him. In a hospital room. Supreme, unique joy. I also understood his patched-up shoes. His worn but clean clothes. He wanted to treat himself to a final luxury. A poor man's final elegance. Convinced that he was living the final scene of a comedy. Or a tragedy. Depending on which loge you're sitting in. He had to die clean, despite his poverty. To leave cleanly from a world that had never taken the time to show compassion for the suffering of others, much less for that of some anonymous wretch. And, above all, I discovered, with a pang in my heart, that we all played a part in this. We're all responsible for the shipwreck of our society.

And Raynand remembers his mother, dead from tuberculosis at the sanatorium. Completely drunk, he stands up. He fills his glass to the brim. Then, out loud, he starts shouting invectives at everyone in attendance.

– Yes, the doctor's right. All of us, we've done wrong. Bunch of yuppies. Bunch of couch potatoes. You get your theoretical humanity from insipid books. But you know nothing of the real world. Bunch of demagogic intellectuals. Your indifference to the trampling of others, you'll pay for it. Bunch of losers! Bunch of assassins! Band of ignoramuses! Bunch of impotent posers! You're repulsive!

General astonishment. Scandal. Unexpected tumult. A scene at once comical and dramatic. Paulin and Roger try to calm Raynand in vain. Finally, they hold him firmly by the arms. And make their way to the exit. All the while, the drunken Raynand spews his invectives, cut short by a single hiccup of rage and anger.

– You get married . . . you celebrate . . . while others die . . . like dogs . . . You stuff your faces . . . you take women to bed . . . while others die of hunger . . . Bunch of assholes in a world of schemers and idiots. All of you, you're guilty of having lived in shit. Of continuing to live in shit. You're nothing but shit! You'll soon pay. Heap of overstuffed, good-for-nothing bastards!

∎   ∎   ∎

Rotten years filled with bad days, what more should I expect of you? My suffering heart counts nearly ten million tremblings in the lazy oil of hope.

I left behind me, far behind me, just short of my twelfth birthday, the little green boutique that sold happiness by the bushel. I submitted the innocence of my eyes to the harshness of the world. But ever since the veil of indifference has been torn, I'm threatened by schizophrenic rage. And all I do is haggle over the smallest measure of hope.

At daybreak, I will buy a comb to clean the mud out of my lice-filled hair, a stiff horsehair brush to scratch at the sores all over my parasite-covered body.

Solitary, I turn in circles in the streets, doors closing as I pass by. I walk against the wind, which awkwardly irrigates the heat of the sun, so as better to dry up the vomit on my chest and the rot on my back.

My face, a mad mirror. My veins become dull. I'm filthy to my very blood. What kindhearted washerwoman will bring my heart to the clear water of the stream?

My brain, a nest of serpents tangled up in themselves. Around me, a swarm of angry bees. I sleep like a woodcutter dreaming of a tree with cut-off fingers. If I wake up, it is only to find boredom lying at the foot of my bed.

Hoping to save the one man capable of escaping the terrible fear, I crossed marshes, rising rivers, virgin forests, desolate savannas, moonless deserts. I ran for an entire night. At dawn, there was only me – headless and heartless cadaver of a madman, lying in a big wheelbarrow full of filth.

I'm tired of trying to hold on to that tilted shadow laid across my path. May the verticality of noon block out the day with an arrow of fire above my skull! The sun ever fixed at its zenith. Only then will my hideous shadow disappear under my vagabond's soles.

The storm has been brewing. My liquefied brains are trickling out of my eyes and my nostrils.

What do you see coming in the distance, daughter?

Broken jaws. A hideous stream of rotten teeth. A horrifying procession of zombies.

The sorcerer told me I should be glad that I have been dead for such a long time. Those of you who are alive have nothing to fear from me. The red wine I drink is only my blood, flowing from my broken heart. I am drunk on my own blood.

■   ■   ■

Raynand sinks further and further into solitude. He no longer tries to see Paulin. He avoids him, in fact. He wants to avoid all contact with his friends. With anything that can remind him of what he has already seen. Already lived. Formidable and painful plunge into peace and silence. Impossible prolonging of a life whose inevitable conclusion would be a dangerous leap into a bottomless abyss. Into the ether of madness. Not once in his exasperated flight has he managed to come even close to the sort of peace he seeks. He only reaches the midpoint of that select space.

That formless land where one's diluted conscience coagulates in a gelatinous mass. Anesthetic. On the contrary, his senses become that much sharper. In a lucid delirium. With prodigious precision, his eyes, nostrils, ears capture images, smells, sounds emerging from everywhere. His heart, having become a ball of fire, radiates intense flashes to immeasurable cosmic distances. Burning wounds and dazzling speed. He suffers. His whole body aches. Henceforth, he becomes familiar with stardust and spectral rays. He participates in the rotation of all the nebulae and all the galaxies.

The worst thing is that all the sensations accumulated from his surroundings assault him with sharp cracks of the whip. Insufferably stinging and bloody. The very environment of the earth heightens his suffering. He feels the beating pulse of the planet. The distended heart of the oceans. He detects the nausea of the volcanoes. The tormented circulation of earthquakes. The faraway fallout of energy raining down. The silent frequency of clusters of light. The flaccid progression of subterranean waters. The spiral unleashing of marine swells. The sharp scraping of the wind. The painful coughing fits of cyclones. The perfumes of the stars, mixed indistinguishably with the smells of plants, make his head spin. Permanent dizziness. His voice, a range of registers, filters the lifeless music of the moon, the piercing song of the comets, the singing exercises of the sun.

Global perception of space and time. His present, no longer reduced to the imperceptible thread of escape, widens into a gigantic luminous band at the limitless borders of the past and the present. Often Raynand strolls along the Colomb Docks. He observes the launching of flaming arrows into the flat zinc of the sea. He seeks out the knives of the wind, closely packed blades skimming the waves. His body, buzzing hive bristling with antennas, picks up thousands of waves. I feel them coming, he says to himself. Bitten by teeth filed down to sharp points. The spinal marrow informs the immense infantry of the nervous system. Rallying the troops. The devastating rise of the river of death. Sudden alarm of the ganglions as they detect the movement of enemy troops. The past and the future blend together. Men stumbling around in the depths of caverns. Pyramids are built in blood. New kings break the gold crowns placed on the cracked skulls of their unfaithful mistresses. The tanks cut the hamstrings of impotent warriors. The temples, the churches, the palaces – they don't even finish crafting the arches of their vaults before crushing them into piles of dusty bricks. All that remains is a few cracked columns to signal that the hand of man has passed through. Sailboats parody the journey of seagulls. Exodus! The earth rolls in an endless widowhood. Nothing but erased generations, obliterated glories! Pitiful little pontoon that will have served, once upon a time, as stopover on the journey of the light, Earth is left breathless and panting with pain.

Raynand, seized by dizziness, stops walking. Seated facing the sea, back against a pillar near the wharf, his gaze bursts forth toward the gaping dome of infinity. He soon falls asleep.

He awakens exhausted. Paralyzed underneath the powdery layers of an opaque night. He gets up. Gropes his way along in the dark. Stumbles. Bumps his foot several times against invisible iron bars. He can't make out a thing. Walled up in a hermetically sealed steel hull. He does not know how long his internment will last. Everything he sees is fuzzy. It's daylight, but thick smoke clouds all the streets. Tangled mass of ropes and guts. A trap woven all around everything by some giant spider. Veiled, the sun no longer shines; it's an eye reddened by viscous tears. A dirty plasma for the living, thinks Raynand. Might this be some kind of bad omen? I must go see Paulin . . . Speak to him . . . Hurry.

This can't be possible! It seems as if all the women I pass in the street are pregnant. But it's true. Even the female animals. What could have happened in the space of one night? All these women visibly pregnant! Bellies nine months big. Ready to give birth. Can they all have become – in the space of one night – a bunch of dangerous conspirators hiding explosives in their guts? Nuclear bombs – who knows? Look at them walking, their eyes haggard. Blind women, carriers of bombs! They'd better not get hit by some speeding car. If their stomachs were to burst!

Raynand walks with a long, brisk stride. His heart, a cauldron of blood, beats violently in his panting throat. His stomach, his own stomach, swells as well and pushes irrepressibly against his leather belt. A bitter smell roasts his nasal passages. He's thirsty. He walks more quickly. He encounters a pregnant woman who looks oddly like Solange.

– Solange!

– What do you want from me?

– Are you pregnant?

– You know full well this is your doing.

– Of what do you so unjustly accuse me?

– It's your cursed seed I carry. Don't pretend not to know.

– But I haven't seen you since our breakup. A year ago. How could this be possible?

– The same way you impregnated all the women of the island, by spraying them with your salty sperm.

– Solange, you've got to be kidding me. What are you talking about?

– About the fact that you knocked me up, Raynand.

– Solange, you're lying. I can't have children. I'm sterile. Encrusted with tumors, nothing works anymore. You know that. And what's more, my doctor castrated me and placed two oval stones in the place of my testicles.

Solange doesn't respond. She turns her back to him, revealing an ulcerated sore on the nape of her neck. Startled, Raynand turns away, his lips pinched in disgust. He gets out of there hurriedly, his temples suddenly clenched between the brass disks of an explosive pair of cymbals. He catches himself running in a street he can't identify, and stops short at a crossroads blocked by a mound of small, naked bodies. Swarming. Covered with bruises. Viscous. Dumbfounded, he refuses to believe his eyes. A sticky pile of newborn children. Strange mass grave blocking the way along a radius of thirty feet. Some are already dead. Throats cut. Strangled by nylon stockings twisted around their necks. Other cry. Squirm. Let loose screams that drive into his ears like so many corks. Into his head. Raynand sees no way out. He has goosebumps. With a start, he goes back the way he came. Starts running again. This isn't possible, he murmurs imperceptibly. I've got to go see Paulin this very minute. His novel . . . I've found the title for his novel . . . The title, a fiery scab on the skin of his book!

Raynand slips into a winding corridor. As he is swallowed up within, his unease worsens. He experiences the painful feeling of being gulped down by some enormous intestine. A carnivorous boa constrictor. Who would have predicted that he'd end up as a pastry crust thrust into the oven of some reptile's's mouth. It seemed as if he were threading his way through some kind of trenches, boarded up by rusty iron sheets. He raises his eyes toward the cutout bits of sky. He sees his own image there, reversed.

The corridor is strewn with the cadavers of children, which he avoids brushing against. What can it mean, he ruminates, this evil spell? This macabre sorcery? In front of him a dazed old man is walking with a comic limp. Once he's closed the three-meter gap between them, he glances furtively at the old man and notices that he's dragging along a voluminous hydrocele that hangs down to his knees. Stupefied, Raynand distances himself hurriedly. Further ahead, a chubby-cheeked, obese woman raises the cloth between her legs. Lets loose a powerful stream of piss. When Raynand passes by her, he can't help but look lustily at her hairy genitals. But under the effect of some curse or other enchantment, she suddenly pushes out a set of stillborn twins. Two little runts coated with tallow, or maybe wax. A bloody placenta. Overcome with nausea, Raynand speeds up, thinking that, whatever the cost, he's got to dig up Paulin. See him. Talk to him. Get to the bottom of all these magic spells. Try to exorcise himself. Finish that novel . . . and come up with the title.

■   ■   ■

A newcomer to sorrow, the widow has a bloody star where her belly button should be. With its tail, the serpent kills the child in its sleep and sucks the breast of the slumbering mother as she dreams of violent love.

Hated Death, pit without bottom, old garbage pail that the centuries can never fill up.

Nostalgia of the river that rushes along, unable to stop at the most beautiful landscapes, then dies at the vertiginous blue mouth of the sea. Hallucinatory visions. Dreams. Reveries. Melancholic revenge on a world gone mad. Memory, gaping wound that bleeds and lets flow diffuse streams of recollections. Noon, a burning killer, assassin of my creeping shadow – give me back my double and my memory. Voiceless actors metamorphose into statues of salt. Though his tongue has been cut off, the whistler carries on with his role. To the very last scene. To the very height of silence. Audience of the leprous and the paralyzed. Lazy toads from stagnant ponds, legs swollen. What happy chance will make you believe in the sovereign urgency of walking?

Stones, slumbering minerals, reason awakens in the troubled waters of my memory. Stones! Are you still sleeping while I go thirsty?

Season of blindness, what a groping track this is, where our dreams run out of breath! And if our passions die out and our desires are silenced, misery is sure to follow. The great blue fear ferments in the solitary caves of exile. Can it be that I've never succeeded in hearing the voice that calls to me? I'd so love to inhale the warm odor of hairy armpits. I won't live in the city of these white houses, pure spaces of solitude. Formidable exile, don't distance me from the stench of the word and of sex. I reject my pride and become a faithful spouse. Sacrifice reclaimed by the long drudgery that goes on and on through the night. Jealousy, hatred, vengeance, petulance, impatience, annoyance, for some time now you've been eating away at me, down to my very roots. Now let my plant grow in good health, in peace, and in wisdom.

■   ■   ■

Right at dawn, an incessant rain taps lightly against the roof. Clouds engorged with moisture pushed along by a cold wind. The sun gives in. The town wakes up late. The doors open only halfway. Through the half-open windows, a few women talk about the vagaries of the weather.

– Such a dreary day! Who'd have predicted such a thing last night?

– Looks like it's going to be cloudy all day.

– It's the beginning of the rainy season.

– That calls for a nice hot dish of ground corn.

– I figured that out as soon as I woke up.

– I sent that maid to the market a while ago now. I've had enough of her dawdling.

– Maybe that's how she manages to get the goods at a better price. The cost of food has gone up.

– Well, I'll bet she passes the time listening to the local boys spout their nonsense.

And so goes a typical conversation among the old ladies in the town's working-class neighborhood every time there's a rainy day. Without sun. Somehow it makes them happy to talk about what a dreary day it is, about what bad weather we're having. But without attributing any particular misfortune to it.

Smack in the middle of the streets, on the sidewalks, surrounding the houses, the wanderers meet up. With noisy exaltation, they clasp hands. Happy as can be to be able to up their ration of raw rum on this rainy day. Then to relax in their bedrooms papered with photos, pages from foreign magazines, places where some sweet forsaken neighbor lives. The street children exult. Play Hula-Hoops. Push wheelbarrows. Stamp at the ground as the soft rain falls. But on this particular day, at around noon, something different happens that causes a general worry to spread. And then full-blown panic. The wind suddenly stirs up more and more intense gusts.

A terrifying winged delegation smacks against the trees in an incredible disarray of branches. Green disorder. Instrumental poem of unbridled nature. Musical writing created out of total uprooting. Removal. Amputation of leafy hands. Raging destruction via the injunction of a new language. The winds cough incessantly. Cough up their water-soaked lungs onto the unbolted roofs. The dismantled doors of the heavens vomit up a load of slovenly clouds. In a confused pell-mell. Theatrical inversion of violence. Profound breach. Deafening blare. In a nutshell, an unexpected cyclone. Children cry, collapse in one fell swoop. People are already talking about the number of victims. And the unstoppable winds tirelessly continue their hysterical pursuit.

Painful embrace that lasts six full hours. Leaving insomnia to swell our eyes. Total nightmare. The streets have become hills of mud. Detritus. Rubble. Debris. Ruins. Mobilized volunteers come and go. Help the disaster victims. Aid the wounded.

In a neighborhood that overlooks the city, Raynand hurries. Runs. For the past month, running has become an essential aspect of his existence, as if he were trying to catch a thief in flight, or to capture lost time.

With as much speed as the hurricane, Raynand crosses the streets strewn with puddles and blocked by uprooted trees. In the blink of an eye, he reaches Magloire Ambroise Avenue. Attracted by a gathering of onlookers in a large circle, he comes upon the scene. At the center, two unmoving bodies. Swept up by the floodwaters of Oak Tree River, they're laid out in a cross. Raynand knows right away who they are: Gordin and Lil'-Pope. Two inseparable hobos. They lived the life of drunken jesters. Everywhere they went they created general hilarity. Lil'-Pope had always been a bum. He got his nickname because of his small stature and slight form. He had a strange and comical way of saying to people he passed in the street: I drink this rum for the fate of my liver and the sake of my faith.

Gordin, at one time a well-respected citizen, had been, before his decline, general director in the Department of the Interior and National Defense. Once very wealthy, he'd spent his weekends in the debauched streets of Batista's Havana. Collected a fat paycheck but spent work hours majestically motoring about town in a big American car. Caught up in some dastardly crime involving money, he was injected with something by his accomplices to shut him up. An injection that made him crazy. His faculties broke down. Subsequently repudiated by his family, abandoned by his friends, fallen from his pedestal, he landed in the slums of the saltworks. In the most rotten neighborhoods. In the generous arms of Lil'-Pope, who welcomed him. Who continues to embrace him. Even in death.

Pensively, Raynand moves away from the crowd. A deep furrow around his eyes. The final verdict, he thinks. Evil must be tracked down through exorcism. Hypocrisy eliminated. Some new space laid out. Evil brought to its knees. All the magic spells turned away. Right there – that's the benefit of catharsis. Following the paths of justice in asceticism. Understanding the trajectory of freedom. The profound sense of things. Seize life by the throat. Refuse to surrender. Never lay down one's arms. Because there's always a break to solder somewhere. A breach to seal off. A crack to fill in. But what is there for me to learn that I don't know already thanks to my own antennae? All I have to do now is figure out where Paulin is hiding. Where he could have squirreled himself away such that I haven't been able to pick up his scent. In what kind of maze? And his novel? The title I've found for him.

■   ■   ■

Higher philosophy of the blade that slices. I entrust my wounded heart to the knowing surgery of the spiders of time. Hands of the clock glide along the canvas of forgetting. Empirical psychiatry. Nocturnal winds brutally read out the sentences of the trees, so sick in their solitude. Anarchic reading. Nothing but a flood of words for so few actions. The river's source only recounts its subterranean adventures to the discretion of stones. Time thickens into the obscurity of absence under the pricklings of impatience. The itchiness of the soul consumed by desperation. I'm still waiting for someone who never comes back, or who comes back different than I'd imagined. Still, I bless the flight of imaginary fires. I wash myself in my tears. I quarantine my sorrow. And then I attempt to laugh from the margins of myself.

False liberty, the glass defeats the revolt of fish in their aquarium. I, for my part, am outraged by the neutral memory of frivolous mirrors and by the blindness of glass walls. I proclaim the power of my eyes over lakes, over the sea, and over all regions peopled by talkative mirrors.

We have lived for so long in a space of darkness that we no longer know the difference between dream and reality, between blindness and sleep. Our eyelids are sewn shut with invisible thread. Offspring with eyeless faces. Neither desiring nor capable of anything, what are we actually worth? We need the light to come, like a brutal army of lancets.

Sound the alarm! Ring the bells. Beat the drums. The storm shows me the depth of the heart. The complexity of life.

Presumptuously, I long took myself for a living god. Beautiful. Terrific. I believed myself to be an irresistible force. Virile stream. Fertile source of light. Powerful wind. Stormy wave churning up the sea. Tossing ships about, leaving wrecks and bodies in my wake. I saw myself as a dense forest. A mountain range. A chain of storms. An earthquake nourishing the veins of the planet with my blood. Avalanche of shattered flint. Burning flame. Devouring mouth. Cutting flash of lightning. Clustering of clouds engorged with rain. Irresistible flood.

For a long time, so arrogantly, I believed I was a magnificent god with the power to single-handedly master the whole of existence. Horrifying solitude! You could even say that I was living nothing more than the weakness and vulnerability of a mere mortal, isolated in his failure. Thus did I learn humility so as to avoid humiliation. I began, painfully, to become a man among men. I suffered. I'm still suffering. But I accept the minuscule existence of drops of water and specks of dust, if they contribute to the growth of the tree. And today more than ever before, recognizing that I am no more than a fragile blade of grass, I shiver like a moonflower hearing the whisper of a nocturnal voice.

▪   ▪   ▪

The horror gets much worse. Recovery seems far away. Each day reveals new wounds. Life in the affected provinces is a long chapter of human suffering laid out for all to see. Deprived of lodgings, threatened with famine, the survivors of the hurricane anxiously await the aid that sparingly trickles in. Growing worry. General anguish. The situation worsens visibly. Desperately.

Unexpectedly, one Monday morning at dawn, a swarm of blond angels appears in the sky over the country. Wings outspread. Acrobatic feats of tightrope walkers. Graceful arcing swoops. Fascinating aerial pirouettes. The angels touch down lightly, as an invisible choir sings a hymn high above the illuminated clouds. The people, filled with wonder, immediately begin saying that God, in His infinite mercy, has sent his emissaries to help us in our misery. This angelic race, according to public rumor, lives in a very rich country in the northern part of the continent. The people of this race are the earthly representatives of his Lord on High. The benevolent glory of Jehovah. The concern of our Lord Jesus Christ for his suffering peoples. They'd take off any time divine assistance was needed in one of those places hit badly by some plague or another, or if democracy and world peace were threatened somewhere.

The divine army of angels would most often intervene in countries ravaged by war and famine.

These winged creatures came in great numbers. Their presence was being felt in the capital, in the provincial towns, in the plains, in the mountainous areas, and even in the most out-of-the-way places. Their missionary equipment consisted of an olive green satchel and a dark brown baton. Rumor had it that they'd be going ahead with a massive distribution of food, clothing, and medicine. And that they'd also bring a special vitamin. An herbal tea for the anemic. An infusion of green leaves. The streets are crowded with people trying to figure out where to find the distribution sites. A noisy, feverish day.

However, at sunset, the people's emotion had reached its high point, such that everyone suddenly lost the ability to speak. Hearts caught in their chests. Tongues stuck behind their teeth. People could only communicate with gestures and signs. The art of miming. Even the elderly, one foot in the grave, had never seen anything like it in their lives. A frightening event beyond the scope of the imagination. A complete upheaval. A horrible and sudden metamorphosis. At dusk, the angels transformed into terrifying beasts. Horns on their heads. Hooked claws. Chewed-up lips through which yellowing, pointed teeth peeked out. Their messenger's batons became threatening pitchforks. They screamed in a choppy, guttural language rife with onomatopoeia. And they didn't hide their hunger for living flesh.

All doors are double-locked. But no one really sleeps, paralyzed with astonishment. Several weeks go by without anyone reacting to the monsters. Suddenly, one morning, over by the Cathedral, there's an unexpected meeting of some brave compatriots who call on the population to get ahold of itself. To get itself together. To move past its fear. To coordinate a national effort to throw off the invaders, the infamous and terrible angel-demons.

Leaning against an electric pole, Raynand listens from a distance to the feverish words of the orators who speak one after another from the low wall that serves as their tribunal. Attracted mainly by the swirling of the crowd, he scrutinizes the faces of the people who make up this heterogeneous assembly. Suddenly hearing a familiar voice, dense with emotion, Raynand raises his head to the stage. He recognizes the imposing and gentle silhouette of Paulin, who has launched into a moving indictment of the wolves who had come from far away, accusing them of having used trickery to invade the sheepfold, the heroic land of the ancestors.

My blood brothers, today we are struck by misfortune and have become paralyzed with fright. Disguised as angels of goodness, a swarm of voracious beasts have destroyed our fields. With their corrosive saliva, they burn the flesh of our women, our children. Full of loathing, they spit on us. Their disgusting breath hovers over the entire island. Strangles us. Submerges us in a hell of sulfur and fire. Their hooves mark our land with the seal of disgrace. We know of no yardstick with which to measure this affront, of no scale capable of weighing this insult, so great is our humiliation. At first, too stunned by their insolence, their hypocrisy, we didn't react. Now the time has come to get rid of our sterile fears. To unburden ourselves of past hatreds so as to meet this enemy with united resistance, a seamless front, a sturdy shield dipped in the courage of the true Haitian.

A storm of applause, fed by deafening screams, interrupts the speaker. Raynand threads his way through the crowd, trying his best to carve out a path through the tightly packed elbows of the heated assembly. He wanted to make his way to Paulin, whom he hadn't seen in so long. He so desperately wanted to see him up close. To talk to him after the meeting. To shake his hand.

. . . This isn't the first time these dreadful monsters have raided a peaceful country. Five centuries ago they came by sea, not yet having sprouted wings. They came with their Holy Bible, which they quickly bartered for Cibao's flakes of gold. Having exterminated millions of Indians within a single decade, they then descended on Africa like an army of ravenous grasshoppers. For three centuries they threw the very womb of the continent into turmoil, made into the widow of so many athletes and so many princes become slaves. In the meantime, they turned Saint-Domingue into an insufferable hell of shame, gunpowder, and whips. The years went by. And one morning, Toussaint Louverture, Jean-Jacques Dessalines, Capois-La-Mort, Henri Christophe, Alexandre Pétion, legitimate heirs to the sun, planted light – an inextinguishable star – in the very core of Haiti.

The whole crowd, in an inexpressible communion, cut off Paulin's words with a clapping of hands, with cheers and deafening cries. The most exuberant shook handkerchiefs and hats to show the speaker their boundless approval. Their indignation. Their resolve to enter into battle. Their faith that they'd win this fight. It was written on every face.

. . . They built up their material riches, their art, their science, and their technology at the expense of four continents. And today they dare speak to us about their "civilization"! Can they already have forgotten that it would suffice to scratch ever so lightly at any stone of their buildings, any slab of their streets, any sheet of metal in their machines to uncover the blood of the oppressed? Citizens of the Third World, any time you pass through Europe or North America, when you visit the high places of so-called Western culture, speak loudly and march proudly, because you can feel right at home there where the strength of your muscles and the blood of your bodies have helped to make life blossom. Your blood converted in the mill of History into Shakespearean plays, Racinian tragedy, Haydn's symphonies, Rembrandt's paintings, and Puccini's operas; into romantic dramas, stone cathedrals, marble palaces, concrete and metal skyscrapers; into Hegelian dialectic, or Einstein's formulas, or launching pads. We must remind all those who have profited from our labor, those secular exploiters who disdain us today, that we have contributed to the progress and the beauty of their civilization, in the mines, on the plantations, in their factories, and often under the overseer's whip. Henceforth, we do not intend to be treated like poor relations and servants. We reject enslavement. And without denying what's ours, we proclaim our right to enjoy all of the West's most marvelous conquests and to savor the fruits that ripen on the manure of our sufferings.

With these words, a real electric current passed through the crowd and it reacted as a single being. On its feet, endlessly applauding the speaker, whose pathos-ridden voice became that of two-thirds of the planet.

. . . Oppressed people of this earth, we need only rely on ourselves. Not even the proletarians of the advanced nations. We blame them, too. In the division of riches between the predators and the prey, they too benefit from our exploitation. And they happily accept the crumbs from the bountiful table of their bosses. For a long time now, they've violated their own pledge, which today they consider like some youthful folly. We've adopted their rallying cry: Stand up, wretched of the earth! But we've remained alone on the pavement. They're no longer by our side. They haven't responded to our brotherly appeal. So where are the cohorts of workers from North America, from the great and sublime Europe? We publicly accuse them of being revolutionaries for nothing more than salaries and social services. Their bellies full of waste, the workers in industrialized countries have become wise adults, drunk on their paid vacations, their leisure activities, their beer and their wine. With their insurance policies and social security, they can hold out for a few more centuries. There's no urgency for them anymore. That's why they're biding their time; they stay blind and deaf to our misery. They aren't threatened. If the body of the snake is on their turf, its voracious head, the devouring head, is definitely on ours, in the Third World. And we should burn down the granaries that feed both the bosses and the workers of the imperialist powers.

Once again, Paulin stops speaking, interrupted by the frenzied bravos of the overexcited crowd. Elbowing his way forward, Raynand gets a lot closer to the low wall where the speaker is standing. He screams Paulin's name at the top of his lungs, trying to be heard over the general enthusiasm. The patriotic fervor swollen with the stormy din of an indignant, highly charged crowd.

. . . People of Latin America, Asia, Africa, of the Indian Ocean, the time has come to urge you to combine your efforts to slice off the tentacles that pitilessly suck you dry. The time has come to track the predators skillfully hiding behind the angelic masks of philanthropy. In this regard, it's urgent . . .

At this precise moment, the crowd is thrown into disorder by some violent, unexpected movement. What follows is an indescribable brawl. The protesters disperse in complete panic. The invaders, pitchfork-wielding monsters, knock down the participants, the militant activists, the bystanders, and the passersby. Paulin is arrested and savagely beaten. His head wounded, he bleeds profusely. His face swollen, he hurls abuse at his torturers as they strike him with ferocious rage. Raynand tries desperately to get closer to Paulin. Suddenly, he, too, is seized brutally in the sharp claws of two of the monstrous creatures. He struggles courageously. But the deep bites and scratches of the horrifying beasts soon overcome his physical resistance. As he's being manhandled, forced to walk, he looks around for his friend Paulin while screaming, like a madman, with a hoarse voice:

– Paulin! Paulin! I've found a title for your novel. The perfect title for your novel.

But Paulin, piled into a van, doesn't hear his friend. The evil wind that's blowing that day greedily swallows up Raynand's cries, mixing them with the yelps of some angry dogs nearby.

■   ■   ■

Leave your lamp lit, well in advance of the eclipse of the dying star. The lamp's flame flickers. What treacherous love does it still offer to amnesic butterflies?

Tongue of flame, the wick lights a message much older than the lamp. Let's strip bare the symbol of the light! And from its flesh flows the blood of living things. The flesh is the burning place of all speech; outside it, there is nothing but noise and cold winds. Words that lead nowhere – that inspire neither running nor walking – amount to no more than a leprotic tongue in a useless mouth. Just as poetry is neither scribbling on paper nor drug in the night. It's the shortest path of distraction from the light, the steepest of sloping lines.

Eyes dilated, nostrils flared, ears cocked, pools of light, odors, sounds. Who, then, could possibly speak of incommunicability faced with the persistence of windows opened on to infinity? Depending on the situation, we'll have to use pity or rigor, sympathy or loathing. It's a question of sanctioning the journeyman's guild of rumor and silence. The flames of paradox. Thus will no weapon, no force pull free the cement that binds hands linked in such love.

Rain on spindly fingers, chatty seamstress. The agitated sea deploys its rows of foam-headed horses on the crest of the waves. The clouds unfurl in a blast of blood. There's where our alliance truly begins. Possessed by all the gods and the loas, I want infinite spaces for my insane gestures, on the scale of my mad horse's blood.

Water only knows how to slither along the belly of the earth. Nourishment and blood of warriors, it stands tall in the trunks of trees. Soldiers off to war in the mists of time! Heroes disappeared while drilling in the inexhaustible mines of milky auroras! Brave women dead for love or bread for your children! Caonabo, Anacaona, Boukman, Dessalines, Charlemagne Péralte, when will the star-fruit tree return? Your descendants march in the streets of Port-au-Prince, Mexico, Havana, Dakar, Johannesburg, Chicago, Los Angeles, Boston, Miami, New York, Montreal, Paris . . . Come back to see your Vietnamese children hold out bloody palms while being bombed with napalm.

Enslaved people! Destroy the screen that blocks your view! And you'll understand better. Rebellious people! May the word be free and swollen with light! May the mouth keep resisting the muzzle! You'll be able to give your understanding. But don't take off your shields. Don't accept any form of servitude. Don't sell your soul any longer. Propose and dispose at the same time. If need be, rest yourselves! But never put down your weapons!

Break the chains!

Tear down the barriers!

Unfasten the muzzles!

Now raise your vertical voices high above the flatness of the day!

■   ■   ■

Ten days. It's been exactly ten days. Raynand is bored in the vast courtyard of a camp that the major general of the occupying forces has transformed into a jail so as to accommodate the high number of detainees. The perfume of vetiver, regional flower, the outline of the peak of La Selle hill, the smell of the sea and the intermittent sound of the waves – all of this put together tells Raynand that the prison must not be far from the Carrefour highway. Maybe in Bizoton, he thinks.

The silence of the night allows him to follow the buzzing of motors. Melancholic progression of trucks coming from far away. They pass right in front of the camp. Then they continue on their way. Raynand pictures the sound mounting and fading along a parabolic curve whose apex corresponds to the very highest volume. Well practiced in this acoustical game, he manages to discern the direction of the cars. At times, the wind brings a faraway melody to his ears, a bit of jazz music in the shape of clear blue waves, smooth bursts. And quite often, in some turbulent interior voyage, he's tempted to build a veritable musical architecture with imaginary notes that might harmonize with all the rest.

Little by little, his captivity allows him to discover possibilities in himself he hadn't known before. He knows himself better and better. Recognizes himself. Birth of the self to the self, which situates man with respect to the outside world, the subject with respect to the object. A meticulous prospecting of the unexplored mazes of his existence. Bitterly, he uncovers resources within himself that have never been used, left piled up in his interior caverns. Riches tucked away in deep cavities. So many years lost . . . he thinks sadly. I've been useless . . . I've been useless . . . never really knowing other people or myself. Useless. Vainly, I looked under my own skin. I didn't even know how to rummage through my own veins, or how to find, along the pathways of my blood, the fabulous treasures of a heart too patient to have beaten for nothing. Today a captive, I am born to the infinite liberty of life; and I feel capable of just about anything. Raynand thinks for a long time and tells himself that on the other side of those bars stands a porthole that opens onto a better view of himself.

Obsessed by the idea of seeing Paulin, he feels greatly disappointed by the fact that his friend isn't locked away in the same prison along with him. Despite more than a week in the camp, he's only spoken to a small group of four prisoners, two of whom stand out: an older, serene-looking man named Ganord and a young athlete whose muscles ripple under a filthy sweater whenever he moves his arms. Raynand liked them from the beginning and enjoyed their company. They spoke often. Too often, even. Attracting the attention of the guards, horned monsters with chewed-up lips, pointy teeth, and contorted limbs.

– They're so disgusting.

– Lower your voice. They're watching us.

– They're terrifying with that reddish hair they have.

– They look like crusty pigs.

– An army of extraterrestrials.

– They give off a smell of cloves and parsley.

– At first I thought they came from another planet.

– I just couldn't believe they were inhabitants of Earth.

– They're hideous mutants.

– It's the bitter cold that cooks their skin.

– They must be from some faraway galaxy.

– Lower your voices, I'm telling you. They might hear us and condemn us to be tortured at the stake.

– What are you talking about?

– It means having a stake shoved into your anus and through the intestines.

– Do they really do that?

– Yes. But they have their own way of doing it. And they boast about the originality of their obscene and morbid ways.

– So how do they do it?

– I got an answer to that on the first day of my imprisonment. They were torturing some adolescent accused of rebellion. There were maybe ten torturers. The boy died. Mostly of indignation.

– How's that?

– They don't use the stake to impale you. They're raging homosexuals, endowed with enormous neon-headed golden pricks. They sodomize the victim one after the next. And they do it publicly.

– Watch out! They're looking at us.

– We'd better separate for now.

– No, this isn't the moment, says Ganord. And I have to talk to you. All last night I was kept awake by the hum of patrol cars and the bursts of machine-gun fire.

– What can that mean? asks Raynand.

– It means something big . . . I learned from a newcomer that things are heating up outside. The patriots are fighting in the countryside for the liberation of the nation. For our part, we can't just let ourselves rot in this rattrap. Resignation and inaction yield nothing. It's time we do something.

– The most urgent thing to do is escape, notes Raynand. We've got to come up with a plan to get out of here and act on it as soon as possible.

– Indeed, there's no other solution, says one of the other prisoners. Ganord is the head of an important resistance network. His presence is needed with the militants to organize their operations.

– We'll figure a way out of here, adds Ganord with a meditative air.

– Quiet now. The guards are looking at us suspiciously, remarks Raynand.

■   ■   ■

As if by chance, right after that conversation, their confinement got stricter inside the prison. Going out in the courtyard to get some air was absolutely forbidden. Like a rat trapped in a cage, Raynand walks in circles in his cell. Thinking . . . Observing . . . There was no other solution – he'd have to force open the gates of hell. Get out of there. Keep his head together for the moment. Wait for the best opportunity. Thus passed several miserable weeks of waiting.

Then one Sunday, under orders from the commander, the prisoners are brought out, one after the other. They walk several times around the yard to stretch their limbs. Walking. Nothing but walking. Without speaking. Without looking at one another. They've been walking for an hour. They ceaselessly walk around the perimeter of a rectangle. A monotonous path . . . Shifting of the hips. Crossing of the legs. Irritating alternation. Left foot forward. Then the right. Outside, there's some sort of racket. A wedding of drums, bamboo *vaksin*,* and chants. Raynand realizes it must be a carnival Sunday.

Left foot forward, then the right. Left foot. Right foot. Left. Right. Completing a full circle.

As he walks, Raynand looks out of the corner of his eye at the main gate, guarded by two armed men. Fatigue gradually overcomes him. First in the ankles, then the knees. Then in the lower back and the spine. Left foot forward, then the right. Left. Right. Completing, who knows, perhaps the thousandth circle.

And reaching the point in his trajectory that brought him closest to the gate, like a wild beast pouncing on its prey, Raynand leapt forcefully onto one of the guards and knocked him out with a powerful blow to the neck. The other guard, who'd just opened the gate to let pass an empty old cart, turned around, completely surprised. Without having time to react, he's hit by Raynand's left fist, a masterful uppercut that fractures his jaw. In the same moment, on his feet, crouched in a position of attack, Raynand calls out to his comrades in the midst of an indescribable confusion.

– Let's get out of here! Ganord! Come quickly! My friends, let's go!

He stands up. Takes a step toward the exit. But snatched by some irresistible force, he stumbles in an endless fall. Weightless. When he

* A trumpetlike instrument.

comes to, he smiles. Painfully, he focuses his gaze and tries to make out his surroundings and to understand what happened to him. Through a veil, he recognizes Ganord's face. The latter holds Raynand's head in one of his hands. With the other, he wipes a bloody handkerchief across Raynand's lips.

– Ganord, where am I? asks Raynand, weakly.

– In the van we were able to take from them, thanks to your bravery. You did a great job, Raynand. We've left the main road. They won't be able to find us now.

– What happened, Ganord?

– You were courageous, Raynand. The man driving this van got you in the chest. We took care of him.

– Where am I?

– In the van. They won't find us anymore. We'll fight this battle to the very end.

– Do you think we'll win, Ganord?

– I'm sure we will, Raynand. And you'll get better quickly.

– Will I see him – wherever it is we're going?

– See who?

– I'd like to see him again. I'd like Paulin to be close to me.

– Who is Paulin?

– My best friend. The one I've been looking for everywhere. I never found him . . . I walked . . . I ran . . . my whole life . . . My friend has always been a step ahead of me.

– Really, who is he?

– Maybe he's just me . . . Me at a distance . . . Me in the conditional . . . Yet, one time, I got close to him . . . I called after him . . . I called loudly after my friend Paulin who fled far away from me. I screamed after him . . . And my unhinged throat only let escape a little yelp . . . Inarticulate. The sound of a broken accordion. The bark of a wounded dog.

For a few minutes, Raynand is quiet. The vibrations of the car pierce his body with little electrical shocks. Through the undercarriage and the windows he can hear an irritating creaking on the bumpy road. Reaching a turn, in a space of abundant vegetation, he asks Ganord to stop the van so he can contemplate the frolickings of a rara band dancing a few meters from the road in the shade of a giant mapou tree with its lush green branches.

Leaning against Ganord's chest, his lips dry and his gaze pallid, Raynand lets his eyes pass over the orchestra. Two drummers. Three *vaksin* players. The great master *samba,** the choir of backup singers. And then the vast crowd of fanatic participants. Devilish revelers. Curious folks attracted and spellbound by the carnival music. Exuberant fans of Mardi Gras. The jubilance of the rowdy crowd. Transvestite dancers. Chubby-cheeked masks. Burlesque heads. A paradoxical mix of slovenly exhibitions, triumphant rage, and macabre masquerade. A noisily theatrical and erotic releasing of tension. A mind-boggling happening. And someone dressed up as a pregnant woman who makes him think of Paulin. Of the novel. Of the title of the novel.

* Composer of popular songs.

– Oh, yes. The novel! . . . he mutters. Ready . . . ready . . . to burst! And with the flat of his hand, Ganord slowly closes the lids of Raynand's eyes, fixed and infinitely sad.

archipelago books
is a not-for-profit literary press devoted to
promoting cross-cultural exchange through innovative
classic and contemporary international literature
www.archipelagobooks.org